D0179962

"Nonsense," said the London skeptics.
"HITLER IS ALWAYS SPOUTING OFF!"

Hitler is boasting of a secret weapon that will destroy his enemies. No one believes him, except one young physicist, Dr. Robert V. Jones, who works for the scientific intelligence section of the Air Ministry.

A mysterious box containing a coded message has led Dr. Jones to the discovery of a small fishing village on the Baltic Coast—Peenemünde.

Though Jones is not aware of it, Peenemünde is the focus for another man deeply involved in rocketry. The man is unknown to British intelligence. His name is Wernher von Braun.

ROCKET ISLAND
THEODORE TAYLOR

AN AVON FLARE BOOK

ROCKET ISLAND is an original publication of Avon Books. This work has never before appeared in book form.

AVON BOOKS
A division of
The Hearst Corporation
1790 Broadway
New York, New York 10019

First Flare Printing, August 1985

FLARE TRADEMARK REG. U. S. PAT. OFF. AND IN
OTHER COUNTRIES, MARCA REGISTRADA, HECHO EN
U. S. A.

Printed in the U. S. A.

WFH 10 9 8 7 6 5 4 3 2 1

For

Jeanne and Stan Johnson

ROCKET ISLAND

1. The Oslo Letter

Oslo, Norway, is quiet and cold this October night, 1939, when a bundled figure approaches the British consular building to slide an envelope addressed "Naval Attaché" through the mail slot. The next morning, Captain Hector Boyes, Royal Navy, discovers that the message is written in flawless German. Quickly translated, the surprising letter is an offer to reveal military secrets of the Third Reich, the Nazi government of Adolf Hitler.

There is no request for money or for any kind of intelligence exchange. Simply, if the British are interested in knowing various German scientific and technical developments, they are to alter the nightly news broadcasts beamed to Berlin to say, *"Hullo, hier ist London . . ."* ("Hello, here is London . . .") instead of, "Good evening, this is London . . ."

War between England and Germany had begun September 3, less than two months previously, and elaborate spy games are being played on both sides, but the British have nothing to lose this time. Captain Boyes forwards the letter to superiors and the nightly broadcast is duly altered. Nonetheless, both Boyes and British intelligence experts smell a hoax. Dozens of anonymous letters are being received all over the world. Usual in any war.

But during the night of November 4–5, when it is all quiet again along the Stortinget and down Karl Johansgate to the Norwegian king's palace, the same shadowy figure approaches the same mail slot with a larger package that contains a letter and a small box.

Captain Boyes wisely does not tamper with the little sealed box and, aside from a quick glance at the seven typewritten pages signed, "A German wishes you well," makes no judgment on what he has received. He immediately forwards all the material to London in a locked pouch.

After routing, the translated letter and parcel arrive on the desk of Dr. Robert V. Jones of Air Ministry Scientific Intelligence. Fearing that the box might contain a tiny bomb, the young physicist very gingerly unwraps it, uncovering a sealed glass tube, harmless in its present form.

The seven-page translation, however, identifies the tube as a new electronic triggering device for proximity fuses in antiaircraft shells. Jones gasps. There is little doubt that the tube is authentic.

As Jones studies the other information in the letter—an amazing collection of what appears to be highly secret information—he is convinced that much of it is accurate, a huge and unexpected windfall for England. He definitely does not believe the letter is a hoax.

There are details about radar systems, about two new torpedoes developed for the German navy, about the forthcoming use of the twin-engined Junkers 88 as a dive bomber, and about a place called Peenemünde where large, long-range rockets are being tested.

Jones is stunned by this intelligence gift from the German well-wisher in Norway. The "Oslo letter" is immediately circulated to top officers and civilians concerned in the army, navy, and air force. It is also quickly and arrogantly rejected by most experts as a plant, a document designed by Nazi intelligence to make the British waste valuable time and personnel in checking accuracy. As fall turns to winter, the Oslo letter is doomed to gather dust.

No one makes any connection between the gift and a recent speech made by Hitler in Danzig, occupied Poland. The dictator boasted of a secret weapon to be used against Germany's enemies. Nonsense, said the London skeptics. *Hitler is always spouting off.*

The twenty-eight-year-old Dr. Jones is new to his job but has worked in the Admiralty Research Laboratory and in the famed Clarendon Laboratory. An Oxford graduate, said to be a "brilliant chap" by colleagues, he takes his work very seriously and doesn't always agree with his superiors. He quickly checks a map of Germany. Peenemünde, he discovers, is a tiny fishing village on a wooded island-peninsula on the Baltic coast near the border of Poland. The peninsula lies off the lake-dotted state of Pomerania, a region noted for ancient political upheavals as well as quiet beauty.

Though he is not aware of it, Peenemünde has long been an attraction for a man deeply involved in rocketry. The man, unknown to British intelligence, is named Wernher von Braun.

2. Rocketfield

Berlin, fall, 1929: Willy Ley is beginning to make a sort of name for himself by writing about rockets and the preposterous prospect of zooming off into space. A student of astronomy and physics, the twenty-two-year-old Ley makes it all sound possible and has the knack of uncomplicating complicated theories. On this day, approaching the front door of his parents' home, he hears Beethoven's *Moonlight* Sonata being expertly played and in a moment meets the pianist, Wernher von Braun.

With striking blond good looks, sixteen-year-old von Braun has just graduated from high school and will soon enter the Institute of Technology, better known to Berliners as just Charlottenburg. He has read Ley's book on space travel, printed three years previously, and wants advice on a career in rocketry; he also wants to join the Verein fur Raumschiffart (VfR), the Society for Space Travel, founded in 1927, an organization held in disdain by many scientists. The idea of space travel is generally considered to be in the realm of fantasy.

Yet in America, scholarly, retiring Dr. Robert H. Goddard, a physicist at Clark University, long a believer in reaching high altitudes and even in interplanetary travel, has already invented a rocket motor that uses liquid oxygen and gasoline. In March 1926, he fired off the world's first liquid-fuel rocket from a small, snowy farm at Auburn, Massachusetts. In all probability, that "cabbage-patch'' rocket was the turning point in man's reach for outer space.

In Russia, the obscure schoolteacher Konstantine Ziolkovsky had been writing down theories of space travel since 1898. He had notebooks filled with complicated calculations that indicated to him that man could reach the moon and beyond.

Soon, von Braun is the happy, unpaid assistant to Professor Hermann Oberth, one of the founders of VfR. Oberth, born in the Alps of Rumania, is Germany's leading thinker on the possibilities of space flight. He, too, has been experimenting with liquid-fuel rocket motors.

Wernher, second son of landholding East Prussian aristocrats Baron Magnus and Emmy von Braun, had seemed much more interested in music than in science until just recently. Then he saw a rocket-propelled car performance in Berlin. Soon he was experimenting himself by attaching solid-fuel rockets to a coaster wagon.

Oberth's latest rocket, tied to exploitation for the world's first space movie, *Frau Im Mond (Girl in the Moon)*, fizzles sadly, but von Braun, Ley, and other youthful members of VfR put together an imaginative ''space travel'' exhibit, based on Oberth's concepts, for the film's Berlin opening. The wooden spaceship attracts considerable attention at a local department store.

Another assistant to Oberth is Rudolph Nebel, a fighter pilot during the Kaiser's war with England, France, and the U.S.A., not long ended. Exuding charm and style, the thirty-four-year-old aviator is perfect for recruitment of funds and materials for the rocket society, which now numbers about a thousand members.

A third assistant is Klaus Riedel, also a student engineer. The trio, with von Braun the youngest, works with Oberth on his Kegeldeuse, the first recognized rocket engine to be built in Europe. Running on liquid oxygen and gasoline, the small engine is ignited when Riedel throws a burning rag at it, then dashes behind a metal screen.

They also work on Nebel's Mirak motor, testing it several times on a farm in Saxony.

With the departure of Professor Oberth to Rumania, there to resume teaching mathematics, his three assistants carry on. They talk and work on rocket design; they attend VfR meetings and attempt to raise money for experiments. They need a permanent home, not a farm field, for the society, and Nebel talks his way into a city lease for an abandoned three-hundred acre ammunition dump at Reinickendorf, a suburb of Berlin. Rental is equivalent to four U.S. dollars annually. The excited members name the experimental grounds *Raketenflugplatz, Berline.* Rocketfield, Berlin.

The half-dozen buildings, some with thick concrete walls, leftovers from ammunition storage days of World War I, are ideal for experimental work. Several are ready-made for safety blockhouses where firings can be observed. Nebel, Riedel, and von Braun often sleep at Rocketfield, working until early hours, caught up in excitement.

Money for experimentation is not easy to come by in postwar Germany, and Nebel does everything from cadging free food from the Red Cross with which to feed unpaid mechanics, to charging admission to witness rocket launchings. Private industry is not rushing to provide machinery and needed materials. The newspaper *Berlin Tageblatt* scornfully says of VfR, ". . . boys playing with dangerous toys."

Boys, perhaps; dangerous, certainly; toys, never.

The Army Weapons Department, under Colonel Professor Karl Becker, had taken an interest in the rocket literature of the 1920s, making a report to the minister of national defense. Not long after von Braun approached Willy Ley, the Ballistics and Munitions Branch decided to begin research to explore the possibility of using liquid-fuel rockets for war purposes.

So one welcome VfR benefactor this year is Captain Dr. Walter Dornberger of the Ballistics Branch, who manages to unofficially supply 5,000 Deutschmarks, about $1,200 U.S., to further experimentation at Rocketfield. For many reasons, Dornberger prefers to keep this contribution very quiet.

Willy Ley names the first VfR rocket *Repulsor,* and it is launched in May 1931, frightening everyone in attendance, including Captain Dornberger. Instead of blasting straight up, it veers away from Rocketfield. Von Braun, Riedel, and Nebel mount bicycles to chase it, praying *Repulsor I* hasn't landed on the nearby police station or in someone's picnic basket.

The wreck of the "two-stick," or "two-leg," rocket is lodged in a tree almost half a mile away, having attained an altitude of about two hundred feet. At that, *Repulsor I* has behaved better than some past rockets. A few chased spectators around Rocketfield.

In time, the rockets travel up one thousand feet, and a small parachute pops out to lower them safely to earth. Countdown from the crude blockhouse is *"Feuer! Benzin! Sauerstoff!"* ("Fire! Gasoline! Oxygen!") But always hold your breath! These machines are never reliable one launch to the next. Toys they are not.

Oberth had long advocated alcohol instead of gasoline as rocket fuel, and Riedel soon advances that theory with numerous tests, von Braun assisting. Riedel's father owns a distillery, and Klaus expropriates alcohol to explore Oberth's ideas.

"A-Stoff" is the code name for liquid oxygen, "B-Stoff" for gasoline, "C-Stoff" for methyl alcohol. Already, a language for rocketry is being developed.

The young rocketeers in Germany are no different from thousands of American youths who are building aircraft models, some even constructing full-size aircraft in garages from steel tubing, hardwood, and canvas. Charles Lindbergh has recently flown the Atlantic, stirring dreams. However, a very special atmosphere exists at Rocketfield because the VfR youths believe they are already beyond conventional aviation.

During the summer of 1931, a number of curious officers from the *Waffenprufamt* (Army Weapons Department) visit the ramshackle, weed-littered field, watching as motors are tested or attempts are made to launch rockets. Mostly, these observers are dressed in civilian clothes. Two stand out: Colonel Professor Becker, head of research and development, and Captain Dr. Dornberger, ballistics man. Though they haven't discussed it with von Braun, Ley, Riedel, or anyone else of VfR, the main reason for their attendance is that the Treaty of Versailles, signed after World War I, rules out German heavy artillery but mentions *nothing about rockets*. Hitler has not yet come to power in Germany, and this is a decision of the supposedly peaceful postwar Weimar government.

Becker has decided to make a deadly saturation weapon out of solid-fuel rockets and to explore ways to produce liquid-fuel rockets to carry explosives, conveniently stepping around the Versailles treaty. Walter Dornberger is his choice to head the latter program.

The balding Dornberger, thirty-five years old, is a confident, tough man, a leader as well as a fine engineer. Serving as an artillery lieutenant in the recent war, he was captured by U.S. marines and spent two years in French prisoner-of-war camps, mostly in solitary confinement because of repeated escape attempts. Returning to the army after graduating from the University of Berlin, where he received his doctorate in mechanical engineering, Dornberger is convinced of the future of rocketry.

During the fall of 1932, he establishes an experimental station at the Kummersdorf army ammunition proving ground eighteen miles south of Berlin. Quite naturally, he looks to VfR members for his new staff, and on October 1 hires nineteen-year-old Wernher von Braun as his technical assistant.

In the past, weapons development has always involved private industry, but this time no German company is interested. Rockets are still viewed as enlarged fireworks.

Becker is actually pleased with that situation. What he hopes to do involves the highest secrecy; to maintain it requires work behind military fences guarded by men with guns.

Dornberger then stipulates that von Braun must simultaneously study physics at Berlin University under a particular professor who is also the Ordnance Board's chief of research. Wernher can use the Kummersdorf facility for any experimentation necessary to write his doctor's thesis.

In effect, to become *Dr.* von Braun he must make a missile, a war weapon. Neither Becker nor Dornberger are at all concerned with space travel, which seems to be the student's ultimate goal.

3. Kummersdorf-West

The army pinewoods proving ground area has the official title of *Versuchstelle* (Experiment Station) Kummersdorf-West, and another key employee is added, engineer Walter Riedel, a liquid-oxygen expert, no kin to Klaus. He is a quiet, steady, deliberate man, good balance for the exuberant and sometimes reckless nature of von Braun. Dornberger goes about building his experiment station staff slowly and carefully.

Three days before Christmas 1932, von Braun and his small crew, now numbering seven, are ready for the first test at Kummersdorf with an advanced version of Nebel's Mirak. This alcohol–liquid-oxygen motor is capable of 650 pounds of thrust, more energy than any rocket tested thus far in Germany, or anywhere else.

The silver-gray motor sits in a newly built concrete-walled test stand in the thick woods. New and special instrumentation will supposedly let the observers know exactly what is occurring as each firing step takes place. Twin searchlights are focused on the twenty-inch motor. Everyone is warned to seek cover.

If anyone is uncomfortable with von Braun's extreme youth on this frigid night, words remain unspoken. He is in complete command of the tests. Dornberger and a few other officers are present as he lights a gasoline-dipped rag attached to a twelve-foot pole, then touches the flame to the bottom of the motor as alcohol drips from it.

The resulting explosion, so reminiscent of makeshift

Rocketfield, lights up the forest in oranges, blues, and whites, shattering the quiet for miles around. Ripping of steel, splintering of wood, and the usual "boom" of any big explosion are mixed together as the motor blows itself to pieces, some of which lodge in the evergreens. The new test stand is practically destroyed.

Fortunately, no one is injured, and while von Braun and his crew wish the test had been successful, the general feeling in the pinewoods is an old one for any engineer—back to the drawing boards. Laughter is heard.

At eleven o'clock in the morning some thirty days later, Adolf Hitler, wearing a black frock coat and carrying a top hat, comes to power as chancellor of the Third Reich. In the evening, at a torchlight parade, the new leader watches twenty-five thousand of his storm troopers as they march by him singing lustily. A spotlight is trained on the Führer, and at one point he whispers prophetically, "No power on earth will ever get me out of here alive . . ."

To one student at Berlin University, "Hitler is only a pompous fool with a Charlie Chaplin mustache." At least, this is how von Braun describes Hitler to close associates over a glass of beer. He'll soon discover that his assessment of the chancellor as a "fool" is almost totally incorrect.

Throughout 1933, von Braun puts in many seventeen- and eighteen-hour days, dividing his time between physics and the work at Kummersdorf. A name has been given to the first complete rocket he is building—Aggregat One, or A-1. All of the knowledge gained at Rocketfield, everything useful written by Oberth, Goddard, or Ziolkovsky, is being applied to the A-1, a vehicle four feet, seven inches long, about a foot in diameter.

Not unexpectedly, there are many more failures than successes throughout the year. Motors burn up or blow up. Lessons are learned the hard way. Dornberger is under continuous pressure for money to keep the experimental station going. Many within the ordnance department still believe that rockets are just dangerous playtoys, a waste of money.

Hitler himself visits Kummersdorf briefly in 1933, witnessing the firing of the A-1 motor. He examines the four-and-a-half-foot rocket and obviously is not impressed. Von Braun, who looks to be even less than twenty, mentions "space travel," which brings a frown to the Führer's face, a reaction not sought by Becker or Dornberger. Hitler later comments that it all seems "amateurish."

A-1 never leaves the test stand, nor was it ever intended to be launched, but finally the motor works perfectly. It is time for von Braun and his team to build the A-2, with a duraluminum motor of 2,200 pounds of thrust, almost triple the power of any rocket motor yet attempted.

Work on the A-2 continues throughout 1934, but the hope of using the new, powerful motor is scrapped for the time being. "We just don't have the money," Dornberger tells von Braun. The larger engine would have required a rocket triple the size of the A-2. The old proven 650-thrust will have to take A-2 aloft.

Von Braun adds pilot training to his schedule during the summer and joins the air force reserves as required by a new law, enjoying time in the cockpit when not pressed by other duties. He also receives word this summer that Rocketfield has been "taken over" by a group of young Nazis in powder-blue uniforms. Willy Ley, still vice-president of VfR, attempts to enter the premises but is turned away. Secret police, the new *Geheime Staatspolizei*, or Gestapo are inside, seizing documents for examination. But VfR meets its demise not because of the Gestapo, but because of unpaid bills, a sad and silly end for the world's first true space organization.

At Kummersdorf-West, there is little lament over the loss of Rocketfield and not much attention given to politics and such radical organizations as the Gestapo. The rocket makers are too busy to look at what is going on around them, or simply ignore it. A pair of A-2s named "Max" and "Moritz" are being readied for launch from the island of Borkum in the North Sea.

More and more, the rocketeers are uncomfortable launching near populated areas. As the rockets grow larger, the danger of property damage and fatalities outside the proving ground increases proportionately.

Only a day is taken from the A-2 preparation for von Braun to receive his doctorate in physics at the age of twenty-two. His boyish appearance and manner do not support the formidable new title of Dr. von Braun, and he finds it somewhat embarrassing to be so addressed.

Shortly before Christmas, "Max" and "Moritz" spear up from the cold sands of little Borkum, both reaching altitudes of 6,500 feet, the highest any rocket has ever gone. The motors each burn for sixteen seconds. As the elated team returns to Berlin, they talk of producing the A-3. Additional money from Colonel Professor Becker and the Ordnance Board is now quite likely.

As projected, A-3 will be twenty-five feet long, with a diameter of two and a half feet. Takeoff weight will be 1,650 pounds, five times that of A-2. Motor thrust will be more than 3,000 pounds. Von Braun calculates an altitude upward of 40,000 feet.

Few critics in Berlin will be prone to dismiss the A-3 as a boy's "toy," and, in fact, many military planners around the world, particularly in England and France, would be alarmed if they knew what had happened on Borkum this day.

Thus far, though the German Air Ministry is aware of the small group of rocket advocates in the *Wehrmacht*, the army, it has shown absolutely no interest in the research. The *Luftwaffe*, the air force, concentrating on conventional aircraft, has even rejected as impractical the proposal of one inventor, Paul Schmidt, to develop a pulse-jet motor for a "flying bomb."

Just as rockets aren't new, flying bombs, or unmanned bombers directed by radio, were in concept stages as far back as 1891. The American Kettering Aerial Torpedo of 1918 was a direct prototype for such a weapon.

On Schmidt's behalf, von Braun tells Air Ministry officials that the flying bomb concept is far from impractical, and the fluid-dynamics expert is given a small amount of money to begin development of a pulse-jet motor for what is to become a robot bomb, the infamous V-1 of World War II.

4. Usedom

For months Dornberger, now a major, von Braun, and Walter Riedel have discussed the need for a new, permanent, and "safe" home for the experimental work, one in which the Luftwaffe will likely join someday. From size alone, A-3 now forces that decision. Kummersdorf-West invites tragedy sooner or later. Also, big rocket motors firing off eighteen miles from Berlin automatically eliminates secrecy. Engine thunder can be heard miles away.

North Sea islands such as Borkum are not suitable because of heavy sea traffic in and out of such ports as Hamburg and Bremerhaven. Additionally, testing will arouse the interest of Holland and Denmark, countries flanking Germany.

Spending the Christmas holidays with relatives in the town of Anklam, north of Berlin and not too far from the Baltic shore, von Braun mentions the need for an operational center and is reminded that his father sometimes hunted ducks on the secluded island-peninsula of Usedom. As a small boy, von Braun had gone along with the baron to a lake near the fishing village of Peenemünde.

Previously, Dornberger, von Braun, and Riedel had discussed the Baltic as a likely site, the enclosed sea offering firing safety and some security from snoopers. Usedom is relatively close to Berlin and other large cities such as Rostock and Stettin. Good rail and road connections are available. The trip up from Anklam is less than an hour, and von Braun heads for the Baltic the day after Christmas to refresh his memory.

Usedom (pronounced *Ooo-zay-domm)*, a rather large, jagged triangle of heavily wooded land and small lakes, separates the Bay of Stettin from the Baltic. Actually, there are two islands, with sister Wollin lying to the southeast. Three distinct channels go out to the sea, with Swine Channel separating the two islands. To the southeast is Dievenow Channel and further to the northwest is the Peene River. Peenemünde, meaning "mouth of the Peene," is located there.

As von Braun slowly drives around surveying it all, the island is just as quiet and lovely as his boyhood memory pictured it. Twenty-five miles in length, much of it designated as a game preserve, Usedom is thickly wooded. Fronting gentle dunes covered with coarse grass, the Baltic beach is sandy white, with the pines marching out to the dunes. Pomeranian deer break across the heather, and grebes and coots are everywhere; swans glide around the icy lake waters.

During winter, no more than two thousand people inhabit the whole of the island, and the cloistered area around the village, home of fishing shacks and little else, would be ideal for the research center, von Braun believes. Seven miles from Wolgast, the nearest town on the mainland, Peenemünde seems to be deep in slumber this December.

Most other towns along the Baltic shore prosper during summer with vacation trade, coastal steamers visiting, often heralded by brass bands. Beer and laughter flow. Southeast from Peenemünde, toward the Polish border, is the seaside resort of Zinnowitz, the island's main tourist stop, with several fine seafood restaurants. Vacationers always go to Zinnowitz, seldom to Peenemünde. That factor is a big plus. A fence across the island west of Zinnowitz will make security easier.

In addition to Zinnowitz, the villages of Karlshagen, Zempin, Kozerow, and Uckerwitz can be utilized for off-base housing. Vacation homes are already scattered around, some quite old. Near Karlshagen is a rather new Nazi ''Strength Through Joy'' camp that can be taken over.

The more von Braun looks around, the more he realizes that Usedom is ideal for a secret rocket base. With a varying width of a few hundred yards to fifteen miles, there is room for a long airstrip above Peenemünde village. Along the shore there is plenty of room for test stands, workshops, laboratories, a power plant, a liquid-oxygen plant, and a supersonic wind tunnel. There is also plenty of room for housing within the center as well as barracks for guards.

As far as the scientists, technicians, military personnel, and families of all are concerned, no one could ask for better year-round living in Germany. The Usedom summers are usually warmer and sunnier than those inland. Winters are cold, but the Baltic is usually kinder than Berlin, 110 miles away to the south. Seven miles offshore is Greifswalder Oie, a small lighthouse island that can be used for a temporary launching site while the center is being built.

All in all, von Braun believes no other site in Germany fits the needs of the rocket scientists better than Usedom, an opinion quickly shared by Major Dornberger and Colonel Becker. It is ironic that they all choose a beautiful game preserve to perfect the largest rocket mankind has ever devised.

On a March day in 1936, Dornberger, von Braun, and Walter Riedel sit in the small office they share at Kummersdorf and talk of what might be possible at Peenemünde if they can obtain the necessary money. Having thought about it for years, Dornberger outlines what he believes their rocket of the future should be: *about forty-two feet in length and no more than nine feet over the fins; range of at least 156 miles; a burn-out speed of 3,600 m.p.h.*

Incredibly, the rocket that is to fall on London some years hence is just about this length, range, and speed.

At the above size, the weapon can be transported on normal roads, go through railroad tunnels and along the curvature of railroad tracks. The machine Dornberger projects will be the A-4, and will finally have the name V-2. The rocketeers now have a goal, and Dornberger, as an ordnance expert, is confident that no nation will be able to defend against it except by destroying it at the launching site.

The same month, General Wernher von Fritsch, army commander-in-chief, is finally persuaded by Becker to pay a visit to Kummersdorf. Managing to overwhelm von Fritsch with calculations, von Braun also manages to deafen him with the roar of a 1,500-pound thrust engine. Dornberger and von Braun tell him flatly that they can build a rocket that will reach London, and that, once airborne, cannot be shot down. *Let us build Peenemünde!*

"How much money will you need?" the general asks.

The next month, a conference is held in the office of General Albert Kesselring, chief of staff of the Luftwaffe. The rocket salesmen boldly go beyond London this time and talk about transoceanic rockets of the future, ones that can hit New York. They also talk about rocket propulsion for aircraft. Almost, but not quite, fantasy time.

Kesselring, too, surrenders.

Later that same day, a representative of the Air Ministry drives to Wolgast in a fast car and, in the town across from Usedom over the shallow Peene, meets with officials. The city fathers wisely do not resist, and the Air Ministry man promptly purchases the land necessary for *Heeresversuchstelle* (Army Experimental Station) Peenemünde, a joint project with the Luftwaffe. The latter will build it to Dornberger and von Braun's specifications.

5. Little Oie

Having said several times that he hopes he'll live to be ninety so he can be first to step on the moon (von Braun thinks it might take sixty years before that lunar landing, but is confident there will be one) the tall, big-jawed, youthful scientist always tries to participate personally in experiments, particularly if danger is involved.

Work on rocket motors to power aircraft reaches the testing stage in the spring of 1936, when the Junkers Company delivers a small, wingless fuselage to Kummersdorf. This "Junior" is soon mounted on a huge centrifuge, and a 2,200-thrust motor is installed. On the other end of the long arm is a counterweight.

Von Braun climbs into the cockpit, straps himself firmly, and signals ignition. He spins around at a breathless five g's, and then climbs down after the whirling stops, pale and dizzy but ecstatic that another milestone has been passed. Rocket power can be used with human-piloted aircraft for quick takeoffs and sudden bursts of speed.

While work on the A-3 continues at Kummersdorf, ground is broken for construction at Peenemünde in August 1936, and von Braun makes plans to increase his staff. At least four of the pioneer Rocketfield members, including Klaus Riedel, are to be offered jobs as soon as the island operation begins. As usual, people, not nuts and bolts, are the priority.

One scientist, Dr. Walter Thiel, an expert in combustion, joins the forming rocket team at Kummersdorf in the fall. He is given the job of creating a twenty-five-ton motor. In his thirties, Thiel is the kind of scientist who forgets there is such a thing as a clock.

Dornberger decides to launch A-3 from Greifswalder Oie because of all the construction activity around Peenemünde, and preparations are begun on the tiny lighthouse island. Needed are a concrete pad for the rocket launch, a dugout for safe observation, and various storage sheds. Soon little Greifswalder Oie, better known simply as "Oie," is almost completely covered with rocket launch facilities. Though temporary, Oie is the world's first rocket center, forerunner of such places as Kennedy Space Center.

The first completed A-3 is not much different from the one projected in 1934. The largest rocket yet built, it stands twenty-one feet four inches tall, with a diameter of over two feet. The A-3 is not only larger but considerably more complicated than its predecessors. It will carry a tiny motion-picture camera, more instrumentation, and is designed to respond to radio commands. What is radically different about A-3 is the control and guidance system. Much of the research has been directed toward that system.

Meanwhile, architects and construction crews work six days a week on the new center. Already, security tightens the minute one crosses the new fence just northwest of Karlshagen. Within the stacks of blueprints are plans not only for the power and liquid-oxygen plants, the wind tunnel, and test stands, but also for assembly halls for pilot mass-production missiles. Dornberger and von Braun foresee the day when the pilot models perfected here will be mass-produced elsewhere.

The whole development will be, for the time being, named Werke Ost, or Peenemünde East, commanded by Dornberger with Dr. von Braun as *Direktor.*

Werke West, or Peenemünde West, will be the Luftwaffe operation on the sandy meadow area at the northwest tip of the peninsula. The airstrip is rapidly being completed, along with support buildings, barracks, and offices. Rocket planes, jet engines, and perhaps Paul Schmidt's flying bomb engine will be tested here.

Island roads to both establishments are being laid, and an electric railway with fast and modern cars fashioned after the U-Bahn, the underground in Berlin, will go to the center from the steam railway station at Zinnowitz. Homes and dormitories, apartments for bachelors and single women, are in the blueprints. It is likely that thousands of people, needing a school, athletic field, hospital, and modern hotel, will reside around Karlshagen, if daydreams come true.

Little by little, what is happening here on the quiet, scenic vacation island is the creation not only of an unparalleled scientific research center but also of a self-contained secret community. A person can, and will in the future, exist on the northwest end of Usedom without ever having to touch foot on the mainland.

Dr. von Braun and about one hundred personnel move from Kummersdorf in May 1937, though the Usedom facility is far from complete. Dornberger keeps his office in Kummersdorf and his flat in Charlottenburg, and does a lot of commuting. Off duty, when he has time, he likes to hunt and work on his stamp collection. Close friends sometimes call him Seppl, after *seppl-hosen*, the short leather pants worn by many Bavarians. He does not have problems getting along with his civilian scientific employees.

The first job, of course, is to launch A-3 from Oie, and a trio of the rockets are sent skyward from the tented makeshift center in November. All three are failures. Thiel's rocket motors work well, but the guidance and control system neither guides nor controls.

Other basic faults have not been conquered, and von Braun drops rocket models from aircraft at twenty thousand feet in hopes of achieving the right configuration of fins and body. The needed supersonic wind tunnel, Dornberger's pet, is far from complete.

To reach a good design for A-4, the probable combat rocket for mass production, a whole new system is needed, and a decision is made to "jump" a number and build A-5, a new rocket akin to the A-3 only in size. When A-5 proves itself to be a good vehicle, then the ultimate A-4 will be built.

There is other progress, however. During the summer of 1938, the first rocket plane, purely experimental, whizzes down the runway at Werke West, then swoops around the field. The motor burns for 120 seconds, pleasing the dark-eyed Dr. Thiel and von Braun, though the plane seems somewhat shaky in flight.

While Peenemünde construction races ahead, this whole year is spent in A-5 research, development, and testing. Dr. von Braun tells associates that there are so many exciting possibilities with this new science that he often finds it hard to sleep at night.

Across the North Sea, in London, in early February 1939, there is also a certain amount of restlessness for other reasons. With Hitler acting belligerent and making threatening noises, the British Committee for Scientific Survey of Air Defense points out that the government has no knowledge of what the Germans are developing in the way of new weapons, particularly those that are airborne.

The committee members have never heard of Dornberger, Wernher von Braun, Walter Thiel, or Walter Riedel; they have no inkling of what is happening on Usedom, no idea that Germany is experimenting with rockets of any kind beyond the small, solid-fuel models that many large nations are designing and testing. Yet the committee wisely suggests that a "scientific section" be added to the Directorate of Intelligence, British Air Ministry. The precocious Robert V. Jones, doctor of physics at the age of twenty-two, is nominated for the post.

It is ironic that Dr. Jones and Dr. von Braun are almost the same age, traveling parallel paths but each for an entirely different purpose. Both are brilliant, and the lanky Jones is every bit as dedicated to finding out "what the Nazis are doing" as von Braun is to "doing it."

In March, Hitler is invited to Kummersdorf-West rather than to the muddy tangles of steel and concrete at Peenemünde. The day is cold and wet, and the Führer doesn't look too happy, though he is tanned and appears fit. Basic long-range research is still being carried out at the Berlin proving ground, but Dornberger counsels von Braun against discussing space travel this day, correctly believing that Hitler will react strongly against anything that doesn't have immediate military applications.

Dornberger displays diagrams and sketches; then von Braun gives the technical lecture. Hitler looks and listens impassively. Even the ear-shattering roar of a 2,200-pound engine, its gasses burning a pale blue, fails to change the bored expression of the former infantryman from Austria. At a vegetarian lunch, he finally says, *"Es war doch gewaltig."* Difficult to translate, the sentence means, generally, "Well, this is grand." The reaction does not seem "grand" to those at the lunch table, though General Walter von Brauchitsch, new army commander-in-chief, declares that he, personally, is most impressed. Hitler departs with a formal, "Thank you."

The rocket advocates fly back to Peenemünde with a feeling of despair. Any program that does not strike the dictator's fancy is in deep trouble. However, they do have friends in high places. In late winter, architect Albert Speer, destined to become Hitler's minister of armaments and munitions, visits for the first time. He quickly finds that he likes to mingle with the mostly nonpolitical young scientists and admits great fascination with the work they're doing. "It is like the planning of a miracle," he confides.

Throughout the uneasy summer, the A-5 is being readied for fall launching to test in flight the new guidance and control system, among other things. Much rides on its performance. Continued failure will cause men like von Brauchitsch and a new important booster, Hermann Goering, the air minister, to back away.

On September 1, most Germans, including those pouring concrete at Peenemünde and those out on Oie in rocket launch preparation, are startled to hear radio announcements that German armies have invaded Poland, that Luftwaffe bombs are dropping. Two days later, a somber Sunday, they are even more startled to hear that England and France have declared war against their homeland. Hitler refuses to withdraw his troops from Polish territory. It will be a short war, a victorious war, they are told.

General von Brauchitsch immediately grants the rocket makers the highest possible priority. The need for mass-produced military rockets shifts from the future to now.

On September 19, with Poland almost finished, Hitler gives a speech in the ornate Guild Hall in Danzig, now occupied Poland, hinting of "secret weapons" that he will use against England and France with the *knowledge that they can't be used against Germany.*

Secret weapons? What is he talking about? Military experts the world over ponder that statement as soon as translations of the speech are available.

Particularly alarmed, Prime Minister Neville Chamberlain of England immediately asks British intelligence services to brief him on "those German secret weapons."

The man given the task of rounding up all the briefing information is, of course, young Dr. Jones, eight days into his new assignment as scientific expert in air intelligence. Jones spends a few days in the city headquarters of M.I. 6, the Secret Intelligence Service, and then goes to serene, outlying Bletchly Park, where all the intelligence files dating back to World War I are stored.

As days go by, Jones forms the opinion that the old files aren't "very inspiring." Material on exotic "death rays," for instance, isn't substantial or substantiated. He studies Hitler's speech at length and decides that whatever weapon the German dictator is talking about must be air carried, one way or another. However, that is just a guess.

On October 17, British intelligence receives a report, clearly labeled gossip, about a "Professor Schmidz" who has perfected a "rocket shell" with a range of three hundred miles and carrying three hundred pounds of explosives. It is reported that the professor is testing the weapon in Baltic waters. True or false? No one at Bletchly Park has the answer.

Then the shadowy, friendly man in Oslo delivers his letter, and that material is analyzed by Jones who then delivers his own assessment, listing "bacterial warfare, new gasses, flame weapons, gliding bombs, aerial torpedoes, pilotless aircraft, long-range guns and *rockets*" among the *possible* Hitler terror weapons. The Baltic is suspect from this day on, at least to Jones (italics mine).

Oddly enough, the Jones report to Chamberlain, via superiors, coincides with the firing of the first fully integrated A-5 from Oie. The rocket has the new guidance and control system, and it soars up to seven and a half miles in a flawless performance. Before the complete testing is over, twenty-five of the A-5s are launched, the first ones going up nearly vertically, later ones slanting out. This will be the mode for the A-4 when it is combat ready, whistling to the enemy in London and Paris.

By this fall, Peenemündes East and West are taking shape. Living quarters have been built. The wind tunnel is almost finished; the Measurement House, with all its invaluable instrumentation, is complete; some of the test stands are nearly finished; observation bunkers are ready for occupancy. A few tests have already been made from the firing sites.

But Hitler, late the next month, shocks the scientists by ordering that Peenemünde "be curtailed."

Poland has been easily crushed and the dictator thinks that France will fall too, just as easily. His foot-soldier's grasp of war cannot conceive anything of value in enlarged fireworks. Though Peenemünde's budget is immediately reduced, the rocket makers still have enough money for some continued research. The center on Usedom grows, despite the Führer's mistrust of the project and of the "mad pseudo-scientists," in his opinion, who are sponsoring it.

6. A Golden Time

France surrenders near the end of June 1940, and a week later Hitler removes entirely the already curtailed rocket program from the priority list of military programs, stunning those deeply involved in making the A-4.

A month later, a resounding no from Winston Churchill, England's new prime minister, responding to the dictator's demand for a negotiated peace, brings about Order #17, an all-out Luftwaffe assault on enemy cities. So begins the Battle of Britain. Though Hitler is confident of pounding England into submission, his generals and admirals do not wholly agree.

Field Marshal von Brauchitsch, still a firm believer in the Peenemünde project, cannot directly countermand Hitler's changes in priority but does control troops. Within a few weeks, he daringly begins sending four thousand carefully picked "soldiers," mostly technicians of all varieties, to serve on Usedom, classifying them as being on "front-line duty" so that no one below his own rank can remove them.

Convinced that England will struggle on, the field marshal sets the following September as the date for mass production of the A-4 to begin, an impossible schedule, von Braun maintains. The A-4 hasn't even been test-launched as yet.

Although the military is very much in evidence at Peenemünde, the research center is being run like a private factory. All department heads are civilian, and von

Braun now has his full team on Usedom, the last of the Kummersdorf personnel having shifted to the Baltic.

The A-4 is taking shape daily and weekly. It consists of four sections. The nose cone, over seven feet tall, will contain 1,654 pounds of amatol, an explosive mixture of ammonium nitrate and TNT. Just below the warhead is the instrument section, a space four feet seven inches high. Below that is the twenty-foot fuel tank section, where the alcohol and liquid oxygen are contained. The tail section, housing Thiel's rocket engine, is fourteen feet plus. Overall, the A-4 is forty-six feet eleven inches tall, the largest, most deadly rocket mankind has ever known. Of course, at the moment, as technicians climb ladders and scaffolding to work on it, other nations have no knowledge of its existence.

By early 1941, it is evident that England refuses to be bombed out of existence and that Air Marshal Goering's promise to destroy the Royal Air Force is hollow. So rockets are put back on the priority list with Hitler's mumbled sanction. Though Dornberger and von Braun sometimes feel as if they're on a yo-yo string, they're gratified to be favored once again.

By this time, Peenemünde center, with upward of ten thousand people at work, is a place of remarkable activity and scientific advancement in rocket research, at least ten years ahead of England, the United States, or Russia. Von Braun will later remember it as a "golden time."

Past the administration building, the materials testing building, and the precision-tool workshop, employing some of the finest craftsmen in Germany, is the supersonic wind tunnel, showpiece of the center, a long, low building of red brick set in immaculate gardens among tall pines. Past the wide entrance is a reception room with an engraving prominent on the wall: "Technicians, physicists, and engineers are the pioneers of this world." In charge of the tunnel is its primary designer, young Dr. Rudolph Hermann, recruited by von Braun. In the tunnel itself, built for basic aerodynamic research, not experimentation, there is a constant shrill hiss of dried air streaming at high speeds.

Ten test stands are dotted along the shore and another is back in the woods. Each has a specific purpose. There are some mobile test stands, but most are for static tests of the motors. The deep rumble can be heard night and day. *Pruf 7* (Test Stand #7), up near the end of the island, is the principal A-4 test facility. It includes a huge assembly hangar, where rockets are put together and stored, certain tests accomplished. An elliptical earthworks surrounds the launch site. Engines roar and flames splatter, but the giant tubes are firmly shackled. The flame deflectors are water cooled. The lights are on all night inside the blacked-out assembly hangar as technicians crawl over the scaffolding.

The young rocketeers are constantly looking to the future. *Pruf 12,* a proposed submarine-towed A-4 launching facility, is on the drawing boards. Underwater launch? Yes.

Visitors, high-ranking officers or minister-level officials, mostly from Berlin, sometimes comment that it all "seems unreal" as they cross the Peene again at Wolgast. A movie set for a futuristic film! Against the background of vapor pluming from the liquid-oxygen plant and the rumble of motors, scientists move around in white smocks, technicians in blue or brown. There are business-suited civilians, leather-coated army officers, sailors off the flakship over in the harbor.

More and more there are prisoners of war and slave laborers, many of whom are Poles, housed in a growing, sprawling camp at Trassenheide near Karlshagen, by the great fence; convicts and Jews from concentration camps will soon be added to assemble rockets. Also growing is the presence of the *Schutzstaffel,* the SS, for guard purposes. The research center is beginning to have a tragic, ugly side, and the scientists conveniently turn their backs on it. In Hitler's Nazi Germany, they have little choice.

Peenemünde, the Berliners say, *is,* in many ways, unreal.

The army section and the Luftwaffe section are separated by a wide road, but the goings-on of both sections provide enough "show" daily to entertain the few special visitors. On the Luftwaffe side, the small rocket planes are in operation frequently. One might see a Messerschmitt 163 scream upward into the air, almost vertically, leaving a trail of brownish white smoke. After the motor cuts, it will make whistling arcs, then settle to the long runway. The special visitor may hear a strange "put-put" and be told, "That's the flying bomb engine."

The pulse-jet motor for the projected V-1 flies for the first time this April 1941, tucked under a Gotha 145 training biplane.

There is seldom a dull day on either side of the main road.

Though the hours are long, the work for the scientists in particular is highly exhilarating and exciting in this space pioneer situation. Even the wartime living conditions are excellent. The summer beach is a favorite spot, and a walk through the woods at any time can be restful, though the peace may be shattered by motor tests.

When not hard at work, the dashing Dr. von Braun can be seen riding through the woods on horseback and is very evident at some of the social affairs, usually with a beautiful girl at his side. He lives with other bachelors in an apartment near Block Four, the administration building. His large, paneled office is in Block Four, and he keeps two secretaries very busy.

There are no female rocket scientists, though there are a few women technicians employed in chemical work. Most of the single women are involved in clerical positions and live in a group of dormitory-type buildings between the scientists' family housing area, Siedlung, and the beach at Karlshagen. They do not lack for male attention.

About now, von Braun's early tutor, Professor Oberth, father of German liquid-fuel propulsion, arrives in Peenemünde after working for the Luftwaffe in Vienna. There is no specific job for him. Still a Rumanian citizen, he is being "put on ice," though he doesn't realize it. Quite simply, he knows too much. Intrigue is inevitable.

Inside and outside camouflaged Peenemünde, security is as tight as it would be for Hitler's outer office. Badges identify each person, including Direktor von Braun, and the badges dictate where the wearer can or can't go. The numbered badges must correspond to a pass kept in the pocket at all times. Guards are often ten feet apart. Barbed wire tops the fences. Savage Dobermans are on duty behind the fences.

Yet secrets are never totally safe, and during this year of 1941 a drunken Luftwaffe corporal boasts to a member of the Polish underground that Germany has a new *wunder* weapon that will bring sure victory over England. The underground makes certain this boast reaches occupied Warsaw, but there it sits for another two years, needing the fleshing out of "where and what."

In London, Dr. Jones occasionally thinks about the Oslo report and the story of experiments at the place called Peenemünde, but nothing else crosses his desk to lend credence to the German letter.

In June, Hitler declares war on Russia, and in December the Japanese raid the U.S. naval base at Pearl Harbor, Hawaii, and the United States is finally hauled into the war.

Germany now faces another enemy, and Hitler suddenly, irrationally, calls for rapid deployment of five thousand A-4s. Dornberger and von Braun can only shake their heads. They are at least six months away from a test launch.

7. Today the Spaceship Was Born

Flight Lieutenant D. W. Steventon of the Royal Air Force Photographic Reconnaissance Unit has his Spitfire high over Swinemünde Naval Base, on the opposite end of the islands from the rocket center, this clear day in mid-May, 1942. He is taking pictures of some German destroyers nestled far below. On the way home, proceeding westward, he passes over the Peenemünde area and spots what appears to be an airstrip on the northwest end of Usedom. Steventon routinely hits the camera switch again.

Back in England, intelligence photo analysts examine the prints and see some "odd-shaped buildings and some equally strange embankments." They have no idea that they are looking at the elliptical earthworks around Test Stand #7. In fact, there is a very large missile sitting down there.

The photos are shrugged off, joining the Oslo papers in gathering dust. Unfortunately, Dr. Jones is not aware of the Steventon flight, and Steventon's handiwork over Peenemünde is not forwarded to the scientific intelligence section of the Air Ministry. Jones has no chance to make the linkup.

About thirty days later, the first A-4, embodying all the mistakes and successes of every rocket back to the crazy days of Rocketfield, Berlin, is ready for firing. Thiel's engine has been extensively tested in static firings; every single electrical circuit and moving part has been tested and retested.

It is fitting that such pioneer VfR members as Professor Oberth, Klaus Riedel, and others are present to witness the launch along with Dornberger and von Braun. Albert Speer and the armament chiefs of the three services have flown to the island to watch the A-4 go up. Already they're bedazzled by the tube of steel four stories high, steamlike vapor trailing from it. A true ballistic missile!

Fueling of the forty-six-foot black and white checkered rocket had begun after it was placed upright on the firing table at Test Stand #7. Electrical cables are still hooked to it, feeding current from the ground supply. In a few minutes, the cables will be disconnected.

Hearts beat a little faster.

Countdown starts at 11:52 A.M., June 13, and a siren wails over Peenemünde. Thousands of foreign and forced laborers are locked inside their various buildings, supposedly for safety. Inside, of course, most will not be able to observe the launch. Guards have been ordered to keep them away from the windows.

Ignition is rather simple. The *Zundkreuz* is a pinwheel, set off electrically, that moves horizontally below the rocket motor spewing fire. The old days, just ten years before, of lighting off a rocket with a gasoline-soaked rag are laughable.

Ignition!

As the *Zundkreuz* spins and burns, valves open so that alcohol and liquid oxygen are gravity-fed into the motor from the tanks located above.

Preliminary stage! The loudspeaker calls it out.

To the several hundred witnesses, all in protected positions, some viewing through periscopes near the pad, others farther away on rooftops, the suspense is overpowering. Those intimately connected—Dornberger, von Braun, Thiel, Walter Riedel, Ernst Steinhoff—later say they hardly drew a breath. This vehicle is the most complicated aerial machine ever built by man.

The motor is now roaring, with flames washing beneath the rocket in every direction. Seven tons of thrust, at this point, is not enough to lift the rocket off. The auxiliary fuels are now brought together in the hydrogen-peroxide steam generator; the rocket's turbine begins to build pressure for the next stage, which takes three seconds.

Main stage!

Flames increase and the roar is deafening. The thrust builds from seven tons to twenty-seven tons and the rocket begins to rise slowly.

Liftoff!

The rocket goes up less than its own length in the first second, but it is gaining speed each second or fraction thereof.

Slow-rise is filled with danger as the rocket is never too stable at this stage. It is only after the first four seconds that the launchers can begin to breathe a little easier.

On this day, A-4 #1 doesn't look very stable to the trained eyes. It begins to roll and wobble, causing the checkered paint job to blur as the rocket climbs into low overcast. No shouts of triumph are heard from the scientists. The rocket is in trouble. It can be heard rumbling for a few seconds and then there is silence.

The launch team watches in dismay as #1 falls out of the clouds, end over end, hitting the sea beyond Greifswalder Oie, breaking up and sinking. Though failure was not unexpected, the scientists are nonetheless disappointed.

Albert Speer, however, says that he is "thunderstruck, impressed," even though the test is a failure.

He is soon to be more impressed when told that the scientists and engineers are already thinking of A-9/A-10, a seventy-two foot rocket in three stages capable of reaching New York. This projected vehicle will be the first intercontinental ballistic missile, with a takeoff weight of 192,000 pounds.

Speer is "staggered by the thought of it."

A few days before the A-4 attempt, a meeting of the German Air Ministry Scientific Committee had been held in Berlin, the main topic of discussion being the flying bomb. A rough sketch of the proposed weapon, with its simple pulse-jet engine, was displayed, and on June 19 the ministry gives its highest priority for both development and production.

To be designated Fi 103 (Fieseler 103) and code-named *Kirschkern,* or "Cherry Seed," the V-1 will be developed at the Fieseler Werke near Hannover, with all testing at Peenemünde. With American strength certain to be added to England's in the coming months, pressure is on to put this latest *wunder* weapon into the air.

A-4 #2 is ready for launch on August 16, a hot, clear day around Usedom. Sunbathers and swimmers are chased away from the area anywhere near Test Stand #7. As the missile rises nicely into the sky in what appears to be a perfect launch, there are cheers all around the elliptical earthworks, but they quickly turn to groans when the nose cone breaks off at an altitude of seven miles.

Dr. von Braun orders the two dozen scientists directly involved to begin testing each component all over again, and to keep testing until all the bugs are out of the intricate machinery. Such testing will take five or six weeks, and no launching is scheduled until the fall. Von Braun drives his people hard but never harder than he drives himself.

One of his brightest, most innovative scientists is Dr. Ernst Steinhoff, whose brother Fritz is a U-boat commander. Ernst is head of telemetry, the complex measuring systems for rocket performance developed over the past ten years. Although German submarines are causing havoc along the supply lines between England and the United States, Ernst believes that even more havoc could be created by direct U-boat rocket attacks on such ports as Boston, New York, Norfolk, and the Texas oil ports. Hit America at home and half her navy would be tied up attempting to protect the ports, pulling destroyers off convoy duty.

Fritz Steinhoff's *unterseeboot* is undergoing repairs at nearby Swinemünde, and Ernst receives enthusiastic permission from von Braun and Dornberger to conduct an experiment with it. He goes to the naval base with a few technicians and installs several mortar-firing tubes on the foredeck, then leads waterproof cables into the sub's control room.

A few days later, small rockets are loaded into the tubes and the submarine sails to a position off Oie, diving to about seventy-five feet. Dornberger is down in the U-boat, while Ernst Steinhoff and von Braun observe from shore.

Soon the firing switch is pressed, and suddenly a rocket leaps from the sea. The world's first underwater ballistic missile has just been fired, another historic milestone at Peenemünde. The submarine service resents the intrusion, and no further development is initiated. Nevertheless, that crude rocket spearing up off Oie was the forerunner of today's U. S. Polaris missile.

But successful launching of the big rocket remains the primary goal at Peenemünde, and another test of the A-4 is scheduled for noon, October 3. Likely dating back to his childhood when his mother gave him his first telescope, turning him into an amateur astronomer, von Braun can't get his head out of space. He orders an artist to paint a pretty girl sitting in a quarter-moon on the side of A-4 #3. No matter the military aspects of his work, he remains occupied with a voyage to Earth's nearest neighbor and now believes it will take much less than sixty years to make it.

Fueling and readiness stages pass without problems this day. The loudspeaker intones each step for those in the blockhouses, viewing through thick glass ports, and for those on rooftops farther away. General Dornberger is on top of the Measurement House; von Braun, Stein-hoff, and Dr. Hermann, the wind tunnel man, along with others are atop the assembly workshop of the Develop-ment Works. All have binoculars.

Ignition and preliminary stages are almost simultane-ous. Flame and dust kick out from under the rocket, and the roar follows, A-4 #3 rising steadily. The loudspeaker calls off the seconds. ". . . 4, 5 . . ."

Tilting begins. The rocket is now traveling east-north-east, paralleling the Usedom coast as planned, past awestruck bathers, flying beautifully.

". . . 18, 19, 20, 21 . . . speed of sound . . ."

There is a shout all over the launch area. A-4 #3 is the first rocket to reach the speed of sound. It is still clearly visible in the blue sky, a thrilling sight for those who have labored so long to make it fly.

At "40 seconds," a white trail appears behind it and there are moans. The rocket will fall, some observers are certain. But it is only a vapor trail, the first ever seen by man, as A-4 #3 reaches the freezing air zone. Then the vapor trail begins to zig-zag. There are more moans. Later, the scientists will learn that this is the result of air currents, not rocket malfunction.

". . . 55 seconds, *Brennschluss* . . ."

The final fuel valves are turned off by radio command. It is the end of burning but not the end of the rocket flight. Resistance is almost nil at this altitude, and A-4 #3 will soon reach up to sixty miles at a maximum speed of 3,500 m.p.h. Nothing earthly had ever gone this high and this fast.

At 250 seconds after liftoff, the rocket is still airborne but is now coming down.

". . . 280 seconds . . ."

A-4 #3 is now in dense air again, and calculations indi-cate the steel skin will heat up to 1,200 degrees Fahren-heit.

". . . 296 seconds . . ."

Impact!

A-4 #3 hits the sea, a green dye spot marking its grave far out of the sight of Usedom.

A cheer goes up. Both Dornberger and von Braun have tears in their eyes. The test has been an overwhelming success. They come down off their rooftops, hop into a car, and visit various buildings, shaking hands with scientists, engineers, and technicians. In front of one building they see the lonely figure of Professor Oberth. Von Braun leaps out to hug his former teacher. Bypassed on government orders, the Rumanian "father of German rocketry" has not been part of the launch team and never will be.

A few hours later, Peenemünde receives reports from Baltic fishermen. A "strange plane" crashed in the sea about noontime, they say. The reporting boats set their positions about 118 miles from Usedom.

More jubilation! A hundred eighteen miles is farther away than von Braun had calculated.

At a victory dinner this autumn night, all officers in full dress, scientists in tuxedoes, General Dornberger says, "Today, the spaceship was born. But I warn you that our headaches are by no means over, they are just beginning."

Talk of "spaceships" is ill-advised, even when uttered by a general. But no one from the secret police is listening in the executive dining room this joyous night. Congratulatory telegrams from Berlin are read, and von Braun is awarded the War Service Cross, First Class, with Swords.

Soon there is another triumph, though it has nothing to do with space.

In the first week of December, the airframe of Cherry Seed is tested aerodynamically while strapped to a four-engined Condor bomber operating out of Peenemünde. Dropped, the odd-looking Fi 103 glides away with ease.

Technicians then install the pulse-jet engine on the rather crude airframe, little more than a steel cylinder with stubby wings. On Christmas Eve day, it is tested

over the Baltic, put-putting away from the launch ramp
for about three thousand yards, a most encouraging result.

No matter how it looks, Fi 103 is really an aerial torpedo fashioned after the familiar navy types. If one were
to strap short wings on a streamlined torpedo, then mount
a stovepipe above where the rail would be, a reasonable
facsimile of a flying bomb would result.

The designers envision a final missile about twenty-
five feet long, with 2,200 pounds of high explosives in
the warhead, kept on course by an automatic pilot once
launched. The fuel tank will hold regular 80-octane gas,
quite enough to power this future V-1 to England from
ramps on the north coast of France.

8. Afrika Korps Generals Chat

General Dornberger considers it miraculous as the new year of 1943 begins that the RAF has not yet bombed Peenemünde. He also believes that it is only a matter of time before British intelligence discovers what is going on up in Usedom. Then the "Tall Boys," the blockbusters, will drop.

He's correct, of course. It is only a matter of time. Lately, fragments of information concerning unusual activity on the Baltic coast have begun to filter to London. Danish fishermen, through the underground, did indeed report the "strange plane crash" of October 3.

Then, via Stockholm, comes word that a Danish chemist working in Berlin has overheard a conversation between a professor from the Berlin Technical High School and a German engineer. The good professor, it is said, talked on about a "rocket being tested near Swinemünde, which contained five tons of explosives and had a maximum range of 200 kilometres . . ."

Dr. Jones, hearing of this report, can make no judgment on the explosives, but certainly believes the part about the test "near Swinemünde."

The next month, there is another report from a "neutral source" (Sweden) that the rocket test site is indeed Peenemünde, on Usedom Island, and that a factory is being established elsewhere for production of the secret weapon.

This report is entirely true. The old Zeppelin works at

Friedrichshafen, in south Germany, are about to be refurbished to produce the A-4; a factory in Wiener Neustadt, Austria, will also make A-4s. The procedures will be worked out in the two big concrete assembly halls in *Werke Sud*, at Peenemünde, and the techniques will be applied in the production plants. Another plant is planned for Nordhausen, in central Germany.

During these early months of 1943, there is disaster for Adolf Hitler in Stalingrad. His invading forces are facing humiliating defeat, and a surrender to the Russians is inevitable. An army of 300,000 half-frozen, nearly starving Germans will either have been captured or killed within the next few weeks.

In his underground headquarters, Wolf's Lair, in the snow-covered, mined woods of East Prussia, Hitler is in a continuous rage and showing marked signs of insanity. This day, one subject is the survival of the rocket project and Peenemünde, no matter last fall's great success. Complaints have reached Hitler's desk charging that money is being wasted, that enormous manpower is being tied up, raw materials being drained; nothing of military value will ever be achieved.

One by one, Hitler calls in the high officers who have complained; then he calls in General Dornberger. None of the interviews lasts more than two minutes.

Finally, von Braun is summoned and stays alone with the Führer for almost thirty minutes. Von Braun speaks with clarity, seldom drifting from the subject. He usually answers questions in that same manner, keeping his eyes level, whether it is Hitler or a lowly maintenance man.

Peenemünde is once more saved from its internal critics. It is not so safe from enemy plotting.

In May of the past year, German General Ludwig Cruewell, commander of Afrika Korps, was captured in the first Battle of El Alamein, and General Wilhelm von Thoma, commander of Panzer Army Afrika, was seized the past fall in the second battle of El Alamein. Now they are in London, prisoners of war.

British intelligence thinks it would be a fine idea to place these two old friends in the same room for a long chat this month of March. The pleasant room at the Interrogation Centre is thoroughly bugged, tiny microphones all over it. Pure and simple eavesdropping, this particular intelligence game dates back thousands of years, when men listened through holes in walls. Perhaps Cruewell and von Thoma think the British won't stoop to bugging two generals.

Says von Thoma to Cruewell on March 22:

> . . . but no progress whatsoever can have been made in this rocket business. I saw it once with Field Marshal von Brauchitsch. . . . There is a special ground near Kummersdorf. . . . They've got these huge things which they've brought up there. . . . They've always said they would go up fifteen kilometers into the stratosphere and then . . . you only aim at one area. . . . If one was to . . . every few days . . . frightful . . . The major [Dornberger?] there was full of hope. . . . He said, 'Wait till next spring and the fun will start.'

What they say in the Interrogation Centre is of great interest to Dr. Jones. Fortunately, this time he receives a full transcript of the bugged conversation. These are not unidentified fishermen in dockside bars nor Polish underground members struggling to pass unverified information to Warsaw. These are two experienced, knowledgeable officers. In Jones's mind, von Thoma has just fully verified a portion of the Oslo letter. The Germans are indeed making rockets; Peenemünde is the area. Bombing is a must.

Oddly enough, at almost the same time in Berlin, Dr. Steinhoff and others involved in the mass production of the A-4 decide to make duplicate sets of all the precious blueprints and of the special tools needed for mass production, just in case of air raid.

In Albert Speer's belief, mass production is not that far away, nor is the first A-4 attack on London. Construction of a giant bunker to house and fire the A-4 to England is about to begin on the French coast. Both Dornberger and von Braun believe that the firing units should be mobile, special truck-based operations, but infantryman Hitler favors huge, permanent concrete sites. The dictator still wants five thousand to be fired.

Although the Peenemünde assembly halls designed for producing pilot models are beginning to tool up, there is no intention of making large numbers of missiles there. These plants are intended only to show the mass-production factories how it's done.

Suddenly, unexpectedly, Albert Speer calls Dornberger from Berlin, saying, "The Führer has dreamed that no A-4 will ever reach England."

"Why did he say that?" Dornberger asks, astonished.

"Because I asked him for his personal support for the A-4 program."

Dornberger is both baffled and enraged, once again feeling that his command is on a yo-yo, subject to Hitler's slightest whim. On one hand, the Führer wants thousands of rockets hurled toward London; on the other, he dreams that none can reach the enemy.

There is also the matter of the mass-production schedule. It is officially down on paper that 5,150 rockets will be turned out, ready to launch, between April of this year (1943) and December 1944. The truth of the matter is that most of the tests lately have been failures.

General Dornberger, former stamp collector, happy hunter of deer in Bavarian forests, sometimes wonders if his own sanity will survive the ups and downs from Wolf's Lair.

Coping with Hitler would seem to be quite enough, yet Dornberger has a visitor this early April who is just as unnerving—Heinrich Himmler, chief of the SS and Gestapo. With little warning, Himmler flies in from Berlin to "visit" Peenemünde. The SS, of course, provides some special guard service but at this point has no authority over the rocket center.

In all the years of research, Himmler has never shown any interest in what the rocket scientists were doing. Suddenly, he does. Why? There is no easy answer, although Dornberger knows the SS has its own special-weapons development section.

Dornberger has heard of Himmler for a long time but has never seen him close up. Far from being menacing, Himmler strikes the general as less than extraordinary in appearance. He does not look particularly healthy and his hands seem girlishly soft. Behind his pince-nez glasses are gray-blue eyes that are quite ordinary.

The general escorts the mild-mannered SS chief around the center. Himmler seems very interested in all aspects and asks many questions. Only twice does he startle Dornberger, once in saying, "Once the Führer has decided to give your project his support, your work ceases to be the concern of the Army Weapons Department."

Then, as he boards his aircraft, he says, "Your work is interesting. Perhaps I can help. I'll be back."

Himmler's help is the last thing that Dornberger wants or needs at this moment.

Soon, an officer named Max Wachtel is ordered to report to Peenemünde to begin Fi 103 operations against England. His rank is lieutenant colonel, and he will form an organization to be known as Flak Regiment 155 W. His job: fire V-1s across the English Channel from the French coast.

An officer in German artillery during World War I, Wachtel worked for industrial firms after the Kaiser's defeat, and when it appeared Germany would again go to war he volunteered his services. He is known for his organizational and leadership abilities.

Zempin, a village southeast of the Peenemünde A-4 works, will be the site for training the new regiment and firing off those pulse-jet Cherry Seeds. Catapult "ski-shaped'' launches will be erected, aimed toward the Baltic.

Aware of the Fi-103 mass-production plans just completed, aware of Wachtel's assignment and the flak regiment, aware of much of what is happening on the various battle fronts, von Braun comes to realize this spring of 1943 that the war is lost no matter how his A-4 performs when it hits England. The industrial might of America and the sheer numbers of the Russian army make it impossible for Germany ever to achieve victory, in his belief.

In his paneled office in Haus 4, he tells a few Peenemünde engineers, ''Let's not forget that this is only the beginning of a new era, the era of rocket-powered flight. It is a sad fact that so often new developments get nowhere unless they are first applied to weapons.''

Dr. von Braun is a brilliant man but sometimes isn't very discreet. Sooner or later, his remarks will get him into serious trouble.

9. The PRU Missions

On April 15, Sir Lionel Hastings "Pug" Ismay, Chief of Staff to the War Cabinet, memos Winston Churchill: "The Chiefs of Staff feel that you should be made aware of German experiments with long-range rockets." Five reports, plus the translation of the Afrika Korps generals' conversation, have now been received since December. The Chiefs of Staff also recommend to Churchill that Duncan Sandys, thirty-five-year-old prewar member of Parliament, be appointed to head a rocket investigation.

Tall, redheaded, quick-witted Duncan Sandys, recently commander of Britain's first experimental antiaircraft rocket unit, has been crippled in an auto accident and invalided from the army. He also happens to be Churchill's son-in-law, and while Dr. Jones believes himself to be much better qualified to do the job, politics and in-laws are always present, war or peace.

Sandys begins work this month as other reports filter through to London. After the successful launch of October past, the Peenemünde team has sent up fifteen additional rockets, a few each month. That much activity over the Baltic could not go unnoticed.

Polish slave laborers housed at Trassenheide, next door to Karlshagen and the fence, have passed additional information via Warsaw, and two members of the Polish underground are actually in the work force at Peenemünde. One of them had been sent to the most secret area of the Luftwaffe section to clean toilets. While walking by a shed with an open door, he saw a small type of air-craft minus a cockpit. He had no idea he was looking at an Fi 103. A crude sketch of what he saw made its way to London.

Then a Danish fisherman trapped part of a strange-looking object in his nets. The thing seemed to have a lot of radio equipment in it; a large hunk of concrete was molded into the nose where explosives might otherwise ride. Probably another Cherry Seed.

Among many now being held, three newly arrived German POWs are interrogated in London with rockets especially in mind. One in particular mentions a "long-range, liquid-propelled 'projectile' being developed at a remote village called Peenemünde."

Inch-by-inch photographic reconnaissance is assigned to the Flight section of the Royal Air Force's 540th Squadron stationed at Leuchars, on the east coast of Scotland not too far from Dundee. Of all the uncomfortable wartime flying jobs, assignment to a photographic reconnaissance unit (PRU) may be one of the worst. PRU pilots invite enemy fighters to swarm up. Staying over the target too long while snapping pictures is a quick way to come down in flames.

Not only does Mr. Sandys want all of Usedom thoroughly covered, he has added the nearby island of Rügen and even the Danish possession of Bornholm, now occupied by Nazi troops. The pilots of the 540th Squadron, puzzled at all the commotion over previously non-military islands, and also leery of the danger involved, are told no more than that "there is extreme anxiety in London about the Peenemünde area."

Beyond the possibility of rockets looms an even greater cause for concern, known only to Churchill and a very few top officials. British intelligence is aware that scientists Otto Hahn and Fritz Strassman discovered the principle of uranium fission in 1938, and that Germany is currently conducting atomic energy research. If the Germans carry that forward to conclusion there could be the possibliity of a nuclear warhead built into a long-range rocket.

So it is doubly urgent that the suspected rocket center be meticulously photographed.

Squadron 540 uses versatile De Havilland Mosquitoes for its photo-recco work, and on April 22 one of the twin-engined fighter-bombers roars down the Leuchars runway and up into the sky. It turns for Peenemünde, seven hundred miles away. Machine guns are usually mounted in the Mosquito's nose for combat, but these photo-recco planes have cameras instead of gun barrels up there; instead of bombs in the bomb bay, there are additional fuel tanks.

A special "Duncan Sandys rocket section" has been set up at Medmenham, home of the Central Interpretation Unit, just to analyze the photos Squadron 540 will take.

On this day, A-4 #21 is sitting serenely on Test Stand #7, in the earthworks, waiting for the igniter to send it skyward. Suddenly, air-raid sirens begin to wail from Werke West all the way to Swinemünde as the Mosquito from Scotland comes barging into the area, snooping around. Everything goes on hold while the pesky photo-recco plane does its job. Ack-ack batteries dotted all around and the flakship *Undine,* over in the little harbor, are under orders not to fire. The plane is too high, anyway. No Luftwaffe fighters are sent aloft from mainland fields to intercept. The idea is to remain quiet and show nothing in the pines and oaks and brown-green strips of camouflage.

At 3:25 P.M., the PRU plane heads back for Leuchars and the all clear is sounded along the island dunes. Countdown is continued for #21, and it soon lifts off, going smoothly down range 160 miles.

Beautiful launch, beautiful flight, in von Braun's opinion.

Though thousands of pictures were taken by the Mosquito, and each is analyzed separately, this first special rocket sortie to Usedom unfortunately does not excite anyone. The six stacks of the power plant do not seem to be working (the engineers were filtering the smoke); the liquid-oxygen plant is not visible under camouflage nets; a steam cloud that appears to be coming from nearby a huge building (Test Stand #7 hangar) is not identified as rocket exhaust. Ramps for flying bomb launches are identified as "probably sludge pumps." The strange "elliptical earthworks" with a big crane and that big building a hundred feet high (a hangar) are puzzling but not alarming to the interpreters. The two big buildings south of the earthworks (the pilot rocket assembly halls) are identified as probably being nitrate plants, likely manufacturing explosives.

The photo interpreters in the old Tudor-style mansion at Medmenham by the River Thames do not know how to judge what they are seeing on the prints. There is no past experience with this type of construction to help them make comparisons.

But from this first special coverage, Duncan Sandys concludes that "a heavy long-range rocket is not an immediate threat."

Dr. Jones, who regards himself as the watchdog of places like Peenemünde, is not at all certain of Sandys's assessment, and on the day he is fretfully examining photos in London, the Ministry of Munitions in Berlin is making final plans for mass production.

In fact, another hint of what might be in store for London comes a few days later when Albert Speer tells a cheering audience in the industrial Ruhr Valley, "Even if the German mills of retribution often seem to grind slowly, they do grind very fine."

The Berlin newspaper *Volkischer Beobachter* headlines Speer's ominous speech, "When It Is Time to Settle Accounts, All Will Be Revenged."

Ten days earlier, "unidentified activity" had been reported at Watten, near Calais, on the French north coast. Photo interpreters saw what they thought was a "large rail- and canal-served clearing in the woods, possibly a

gravel pit.'' What they cannot know at this point is that
the ''clearing in the woods'' is the start of the huge A-4
bunker Hitler desires. The walls will be thirty-five to
forty feet thick; connecting tunnels will run thousands of
feet; the bunker will contain almost as much concrete as
Boulder Dam. The Watten photos are filed as ''gravel
pits,'' being of no military threat.

At this rate, the danger of Peenemünde's exposure
from the air is not nearly as great as from within the dog-
patrolled chain link fence. Among the many mistakes
that Germany has made since 1939 has been the annexing
of tiny neutral Luxembourg, forcing its people to become
citizens of the Third Reich. Unhappy Luxembourgers are
now serving in the Wehrmacht or the Luftwaffe; some
are in construction camps such as the one at Peenemünde. Some have already served their work terms and
have been allowed to return home.

One returnee contacts his father, who is a member of
the Belgian underground, and describes the large rockets
being tested on Usedom. Another ex-worker not only describes the rockets but provides sketches of the launch
areas and other installations.

On June 4, Dr. Jones examines the drawings, reads the
rocket descriptions, and comes to a firm conclusion, different from the one reached by the Sandys group: *What is
occurring at Peenemünde is a direct threat.* Now!

Photos from Sortie N/853, June 12, first go to Medmenham and again reveal nothing of an alarming nature
to the interpreters. Five days later a set arrives on Jones's
desk, and he assumes that the experts in the old mansion
have already examined every minute speck on them. Yet
he takes a magnifying glass to double-check. Suddenly,
he spots an object on a railway-type bed that appears to
be about thirty-five feet long, maybe five in diameter.
The object has fins. *A rocket!* At last.

''I experienced the kind of pulse of elation that you get
when after hours of casting you realize a salmon has

taken your line—especially when someone else has had an exhaustive first chance at the pool,'' he later said.

Still, there are people in high places—including Churchill's own personal scientific adviser, Lord Cherwell, a stuffy, stubborn, jealous man—who disagree. Cherwell, the former tutor of Dr. Jones, discounts the object's being a rocket. However, Duncan Sandys is completely convinced, and the interpreters at Medmenham now admit they overlooked the object on the railway bed.

June 24 is a perfect day in the western Baltic, and another PRU sortie is flown from Leuchars, piloted by Flight Sergeant E.P.H. Peek; this time, few can argue that what is clearly visible at Peenemünde is not a rocket. Two, in fact, are perched down there.

In addition to the pair of rockets, Flight Officer Constance Babington-Smith finds four small ''aircraft'' on the photos that have a different configuration from anything she's ever seen before. They leave behind a ''curious trail of dark streaks.'' V-1s. Indeed, Peenemünde is an interesting place, as Heinrich Himmler had said.

Gathering all the rocket information dating back to the Oslo letter, Duncan Sandys completes his investigation on the morning of June 26 and discusses the possible/probable size of the missiles that afternoon with Jones, who makes a guess they may weigh as much forty tons. Others figure up to eighty tons. Either size indicates the capacity for great destruction.

A full meeting of the War Cabinet is called for 10:00 P.M., June 29, in the underground conference room at famed Whitehall in the heart of bomb-blasted London. In addition to Churchill, seated around the room this night are Deputy Prime Minister Clement Attlee, Foreign Secretary Sir Anthony Eden, Lord Beaverbook, who'd seen to it that England had enough aircraft to turn back the Luftwaffe, and others, including the commanders of the three military services. Also attending are Sandys, Lord Cherwell, and the lowest-ranked—but perhaps most important—man for this occasion, Dr. Robert Jones, youngest in the room. Few wartime meetings draw the raw power of this one.

Sandys delivers his report, declaring with certainty that rocket research is going on at Peenemünde, and predicting a shocking estimate of up to four thousand casualties from the direct hit of even one rocket.

Churchill then requests Lord Cherwell to comment on the situation. Cherwell says he thinks the whole long-range rocket situation is a hoax to divert attention from attacks by pilotless bombers. He also estimates that the rockets shown on the photos are wooden dummies.

Churchill listens to his personal adviser and then requests Jones to "tell the truth!" Insisting that he believes that the rocket are genuine, Jones proceeds to refute most of what his stuffy former teacher at Clarendon Lab has to say.

The prime minister does not take long in ordering saturation bombing of the Peenemünde area of Usedom Island.

10. Wolf's Lair

The same day that Duncan Sandys prepares for his night meeting with England's leaders, SS Reichsführer Himmler returns to Usedom Island, driving his own tiny armored car. And while Churchill is asking pertinent questions of Dr. Jones in the underground conference room, Himmler is delivering a five-hour after-dinner discourse to Dornberger, von Braun, and top scientists at Peenemünde.

Himmler discusses the philosophy and purposes of war, then stays overnight in a guest apartment to witness a perfect firing of an A-4 the next day. A visit from the SS chief is always disquieting. On departure, Himmler tells Dornberger he is going to intercede personally with Hitler on behalf of the rocket center. But what are his motives?

Recently promoted to major general, Dornberger replies politely that "we are always pleased to have support," but he has the distinct feeling that Himmler is already trying to add Peenemünde to his area of command. The little armored car drives off toward the red brick tower of Wolgast Cathedral.

Several unsettling events have occurred since Himmler's last visit. The SS is constructing and will administer the underground mass-production factory southeast of Nordhausen in the Harz Mountains. "Administration" means considerable use of concentration camp laborers, and such a camp, to be called Dora, is nearly completed at Kohnstein Mountain. Two parallel tunnels, each a half mile long, forty feet high, and forty feet wide, are being cored out. Assembly lines using political, slave, and POW labor are to produce nine hundred missiles a month. This plant will be called *Mittelwerke*, or Center Plant, and parts of it have already been tunneled for previous commercial use for gasoline storage. Mittelwerke will be the largest underground factory ever built anywhere.

Dornberger doesn't know Colonel Hans Kammler, the man given the construction assignment, but hears that Kammler is laying out ten miles of tunnels, chambers, and galleries connected to a potash mine. He plans an underground liquid-oxygen plant—in fact, a whole complex of underground factories. Hans Kammler has a reputation as the builder of the concentration camp at Buchenwald.

The week after the Himmler visit, Albert Speer calls General Dornberger to summon him, along with von Braun and Ernst Steinhoff, to Wolf's Lair. They are to bring any films, models, still photos, and documents that will boost the A-4 project. Dornberger wonders if the SS chief had arranged the meeting but doesn't ask.

The first time that Dornberger and von Braun had ever seen Adolf Hitler close up was in March 1939, at Kummersdorf-West. He looked tan and fit that day. Now he appears drawn—skin pale, shoulders hunched, eyes dull. Old! A black cape is over his shoulders.

The room is darkened, and the flight of October 3 is screened, with von Braun providing the commentary. As the lights come up, Hitler quickly crosses, cape flowing, to shake Dornberger's hand, saying, ''Why was it that I could not believe in the success of your work? If we'd had those rockets in 1939, we'd never have had this war.''

He is shown models of the *Vidalwagen*, which will transport the missile, and the *Meillerwagen*, which will erect it with the hydraulic boom, placing it on the firing table. He is shown a model of the huge concrete permanent

A-4 firing and storage bunker at Watten, under construction.

Suddenly, eyes lit up, Hitler talks of a "ten-ton warhead," an impossibility in the 1940s.

Then he says animatedly, "What I want is annihilation . . ."

As Steinhoff pilots the trio back to Peenemünde West, the research center has again been given the highest military priority, along with, at last, Hitler's personal and unqualified blessing. But the dictator's call for "annihilation" brings up the old conflict of scientific goals versus those of war. The scientists are committed to the war effort, and whatever personal feelings they have about it often go unspoken. They must do their jobs and hope that their work will be meaningful in peace.

11. Hydra

Code-named Hydra (after the legendary Greek marsh serpent with nine heads, each capable of producing two more when hacked off), the Royal Air Force raid on Peenemünde is targeted not only to destroy the research center but to kill as many scientists and technicians as possible. Never before in modern British warfare have civilians been specifically targeted in operational orders.

Housing areas are very clear on the 540th Squadron's photos, and it is hoped they will be wiped out by explosions. Rocket tooling can be redone, buildings and test stands can be reconstructed, but the Dornbergers, von Brauns, Thiels, Steinhoffs, and Riedels cannot be easily replaced. None are known by name, of course. Bombs are not selective, anyway.

What reaches approval is one massive, low level, extremely dangerous moonlight attack, hitting the rocket center after midnight when most people are asleep.

The attack is to take place "at the first favorable opportunity"—so orders Air Marshal Sir Arthur Harris, chief of Bomber Command, from his headquarters at High Wycombe near Oxford. The fifty-one-year-old career officer, known as "Bomber," has developed many new techniques. The previous year, to aid pilots and bomb aimers, a Pathfinder force had been established by Harris for (1) locating and illuminating the target and marking the aiming points, (2) building up illumination around the aiming points by using "fireraisers," and (3) directing the main bomber force to targets with maximum possible accuracy.

Bomber Harris is a believer in high-level precision attack in daylight and comparatively low-level "area" bombing at night.

"This attack would have to be made in moonlight; there could be no trusting only to H2S [radar] for the identification and marking of a target of this nature," he later recalled.

Bomber Command does not usually send aircraft over Germany during moonlight periods because it is almost suicidal. Nazi night fighters can operate with greater ease against the big planes than in daylight. At night, machine gunners in the bombers have greater difficulty in tracking and hitting the fleeting Messerschmitts and Focke-Wulfs.

Full summer moon will arrive in mid-August, making it easier for the illuminating and marking Pathfinder planes to see the targets, but making it deadly for the bombers.

Detailed operation planning begins at Bomber Command, located beneath a grassy mound and deep layers of concrete: Six hundred heavy bombers—big Handley-Page Halifaxes, Avro Lancasters, and outdated Stirlings—each carrying up to 14,000 pounds of bombs, will fly Hydra. These three types are among the world's largest aircraft.

The Lancaster, for instance, has a wingspan of 102 feet, fuselage length of 69 feet, and stands 20 feet off the ground. Maximum range is 1,660 miles and top speed is 287 m.p.h. at 11,500 feet. The ceiling of the Lancaster is 24,000 feet, but they've been forced above that level by German fighters.

Hoping to avoid a turkey shoot, Bomber Command has planned a diversionary raid of eight Mosquito fighter-bombers over Berlin the night of Hydra. They'll follow the usual "Baltic southern" route to the capital. Any indication that Berlin is about to be bombed arouses fighters from throughout Germany and the nearby occupied countries. They beeline to protect their stately seat of government. Bomber Command hopes they'll respond this exact way the night of Hydra, staying clear of Peenemünde. If the deception fails, slaughter under the Baltic moon may result.

The High Wycombe planners also hope to keep the Luftwaffe defenders stirred up by sending three small groups of raiding Mosquitoes to Berlin on three nights preceding Hydra, all using the same Baltic route, all bypassing Peenemünde as if the place didn't exist.

After recent heavy RAF raids on Ruhr Valley factories and almost total devastation of the huge seaport of Hamburg, British propaganda speeches have threatened repeatedly, "Berlin is next!" Sir Arthur Harris fervently hopes that the Germans will believe this false intimidation. Threats and propaganda aside, there is nothing false about Hydra.

A "Master Bomber," a special officer to circle the target areas, direct traffic, and advise on illumination, marking, and bomb drops, will be used for the first time in an operation of this magnitude. In effect, he will be a "master of explosive ceremonies," a circus ringmaster orbiting above the rocket center.

Chosen for this crucial job is Group Captain John W. Searby, the handsome thirty-year-old commanding officer of the 83rd Squadron, Pathfinders. He's flown about fifty bombing missions so far, including a recent experimental Master Bomber session over Italy. Widely known for his coolness under fire, Searby's voice on the radio to bomber pilots and aimers will likely be calm and reassuring.

Among the Pathfinder bag of tricks will be the use of new "red fire spots," illumination bombs, over the target. These 250-pound bomb cases are packed with impregnated cotton wool that will burn a violent red for about ten minutes, bursting at 3,000 feet. Sixteen of the Pathfinders will be carrying these special loads. Others will have red, green, yellow, and white "indicator" flares so that the bombers, following behind, will hit specific targets.

Round trip to Peenemünde via the North Sea, Denmark, and the western Baltic is about 1,250 miles, which means the aircraft will be aloft seven or eight hours, depending on the locations of their home fields in England. Encounters with night fighters, searchlights, and ack-ack fire are not likely until they reach the "neck" of Denmark.

To confuse enemy radar operators, window—metallic paper strips—will be dropped when the aircraft come within range of Danish shore stations and the large island of Rügen, northwest of Usedom. Dumped by the thousands, shimmering slowly down, window will jam and confuse radar sets both on the ground and in the cockpits of the enemy night fighters.

Training for Hydra, one of the largest raids of the war, begins at bomber bases throughout England. An area of British coast that closely resembles Usedom becomes a "target" for practice runs of the four Pathfinder squadrons under Searby. Residents have no idea why the big planes are roaring overhead three or four days a week.

Pilots and crews are told little beyond that "some specialized radar equipment" is being made on Usedom. Destruction of radar is always an incentive for bomber crews to do a good job.

Photographs and maps are studied. Seventy-nine buildings, mostly small, are counted around the "central area" (Experimental Station). Careful study of the camouflage reveals many things. A scale model of Peenemünde, extending southeast to past Karlshagen, is built, showing the various buildings and the landmarks such as the lakes and the airstrip.

Target areas will be the cluster of experimentation buildings including the area near the wind tunnel extending back to the Test Stand #7, the two big rocket assembly buildings of Werke Süd, and especially the

Siedlung housing area where the scientists and their families will be slumbering when air-raid sirens go off.

There is no plan to attack the Luftwaffe installations around the airstrip. Photos haven't revealed any priority targets there. No one knows the V-1 exists.

12. A Lovely Day

August 17, 1943, dawns quietly with warmth and sunshine at Usedom, but the weather is not so nice at High Wycombe. It is on the gray side there, where Bomber Harris receives his first report for the western Baltic. There'll likely be gentle, feathery stratocumulus clouds high over Peenemünde this night, and a nearly full moon. Perfect!

As of breakfast time, it certainly looks to be a "bomber's moon" if the weather holds. An aircraft will be sent northeast later in the day for a final check, but for the moment Operation Hydra is given the go-ahead. Heavy bomber groups are notified.

By this mid-August, over seventeen thousand people are involved in the work at Peenemünde, twelve hundred having reported within the past two weeks, and although many commute from surrounding towns and villages either on Usedom or the mainland, roughly ten or twelve thousand personnel—scientists, engineers, technicians of all varieties, families, single women, Wehrmacht officers and enlisted men, Luftwaffe personnel, foreign workers, POWs, convicts, political prisoners, SS guards —are estimated to live within the fenced areas or just outside.

Were it not for the war and fences and guards and prisoners Peenemünde could be any industrial park in the suburbs, an ideal place to live and work. Of course, the misery of the labor camps remains hidden behind the glit-

ter of rocket research. Within the past year, this group
has grown at a larger rate than any other.

This pretty morning is like most others at Zinnowitz
Station. Between six and seven o'clock—rush hour—
trains arrive constantly from Swinemünde and Wolgast;
many workers arrive by bicycle. All of them hurry off to
catch the electric going on into the rocket works and the
Luftwaffe section.

If they work at the wind tunnel, they hurry from the
Zinnowitz terminal over to the Werkes Bahnhof—a short
walk—show their passes to the guard, and soon board
modern *Schnellbahn* electric cars that run northwestward
on a single track through the woods.

The village of Trassenheide is first, but only special
trains stop there, then click on by. Just outside Trassenheide is the huge worker camp surrounded by high chain
link fences, barbed wire rolled on top. SS guards are visible. The gray-green wooden barracks and flimsy huts
house an estimated eight to ten thousand males from
occupied eastern countries, some from Germany. Included here are a number of inmates, some of whom are
Jewish, in striped "pajamas."

Next is Karlshagen, tucked into the trees, and just beyond this town is a barracks-type living area for some of
the several thousand army technicians assigned to Peenemünde.

Not far inside the Karlshagen fence, stretching from
the Peene River to the Baltic, is the Siedlung, the housing
estates, spread in rows behind an imposing administra-
tive gate building with a Nazi swastika embedded in the
facing. Inside here, the streets are all formally named and
well landscaped. Married senior scientists live on posh
Hindenburgstrasse in three-story stucco buildings. Less-
er scientists and engineers live on Schulstrasse and Strand-
strasse.

On the other side of the road, which continues on into
the heart of the center and along the rows of test stands
and down toward the beach, are the dormitories for single

women, with the Kameradschaftsheim, once a hotel, the favorite gathering spot. Women are not permitted to live in any of the work areas.

Continuing on northwest, the road loops around the two massive halls of the pilot rocket plants, where mass production will be worked out. Another group of concentration camp prisoners are here in Werke Süd, quickly identified by their pajamas. These men will be employed in rocket assembly.

Luckiest of all tonight, perhaps, will be three-hundred-odd Russian officers who do blueprint work and live in a camp at Wolgast. They will watch the fireworks from afar, as will those at Luftwaffe West.

Though Usedom is on the air-raid path to Berlin, the western Baltic sometimes being a staging area for inland strikes, not many Peenemünders appear to worry too much about falling bombs. They feel rather safe hidden in the woods. Swinemünde has been hit several times, but the planes have always ignored the northwest part of the island.

Within the past week, however, General Dornberger has been warned that an attack is imminent and workmen have been busy digging trenches and covering them with concrete slabs. Though there is a civil defense plan, with designated air-raid wardens, much of it is quite loose and unorganized, unusual for the Germans. There are a few bunkers and some flimsy split-trench shelters; basements in the Siedlung are marked for shelter. Not much else is ready for an air raid.

For the past three nights, sirens have howled, but the British planes have flown on past toward Berlin, and the sirens seem to have been crying wolf.

By 10:00 A.M. this day, swimmers and sunbathers, those off duty, and mothers with children dot the beach. A light breeze is blowing but humidity is still high.

An A-4 is scheduled for liftoff, but technical difficulties arise and the event is scrubbed. Instead of that excitement, a meeting is scheduled for the afternoon. The vexing subject: mass production. The scientists and engineers aren't ready for it, but that doesn't make much difference. Additionally, though the British don't know it yet, they've already struck the first blow at the rocket program. Bombing the Zeppelin works at Friedrichshafen, the British think they've destroyed radar manufacturing. In fact, they've destroyed A-4 mass assembly works, and now some of the rockets will have to be manufactured at Peenemünde as well as in the Harz Mountain tunnels and in Austria.

The meeting, presided over by Dornberger, doesn't go well, and tempers, including von Braun's, flare. No matter what Hitler, Himmler, Speer, and Goering want, the A-4 isn't ready for mass production.

So go the morning and afternoon, a period in which the RAF bombers are being checked, armed, and fueled at such fields as Wyton, Graveley, Little Snoring, Binbrook, Wickenby, Holme-On-Spalding-Moor, and West Wickham—names so harmless, so peaceful, so typically British.

Though there has been no coordination with the Americans for bombing raids this day, the U.S. Eighth Air Force will soon hit Schweinfurt, a ball-bearing center, and Regensburg, an aircraft center, with 376 Flying Fortresses. A very fortunate circumstance, Bomber Harris believes. The massive raids will occupy Luftwaffe minds for a while. He reasons that the Germans will not expect three massive raids within twelve hours.

Briefings begin in midafternoon. The Pathfinder crews hear about the objective of the raid and the Usedom defenses from the intelligence officer; signals and gunnery officers explain procedures of their specialties; weather en route and over the target is briefed by meteorology; the navigation officer talks about route and time schedule.

The crews are flatly told that Bomber Harris has said that if the target is not destroyed, everyone will have to return again and again, beginning the very next night, to do the job properly. No sane member of a bomber crew ever wants to return over *any* target.

The crews see that the route is over the North Sea, over Denmark, over Danish islands, then Rügen, ending at that place called Peenemünde, of which they've never heard. The mystery surrounding it makes it all the more frightening, though intelligence swears that it is lightly defended.

As the afternoon moves along, weather still holding, the eight Mosquitoes of the 139th Squadron fly from their home base at Wyton up to Swanton Morley prior to topping off fuel for the diversionary attack on Berlin, code-named Whitebait.

13. In Flight

Famed woman test pilot Hanna Reitsch, only civilian
ever to be awarded the Iron Cross, Germany's top medal,
is temporarily stationed at Peenemünde West to "wring
out" the new rocket planes. She accepts an invitation this
evening to dine with General Dornberger, von Braun,
and Ernst Steinhoff. Following the afternoon's frustrat-
ing meeting, the scientists find it pleasant to change the
subject from mass production and find out what's happening with the air force across the way. Reitsch will
test-fly the world's fastest plane tomorrow.

At this latitude, in summer, light lingers on. In June,
there are only a few hours of darkness. In August, the
night is longer but there is still daylight well after working hours. Many people are still out on the beach at nine
o'clock. Children are still out playing at the Siedlung.
Former residents remember August 17 as one of the finest days of summer.

Workers are inside various buildings, of course. Night
shifts depend on priority assignments of individual de-
partments.

German time is an hour advanced over England's.

Adolf Hitler is still in Wolf's Lair this evening, but
most of the other Nazi bigwigs are in the capital. Among
those at home along the elegant Kurfurstendamm and
Potsdam Square and the monumental Brandenburg Gate
(despite the war, Berlin remains a city of beauty) are Air
Minister Hermann Goering; Heinrich Himmler, the SS

leader; Dr. Josef Goebbels, the propaganda minister; Albert Speer; and a host of generals. Mrs. Dornberger is in the Charlottenburg flat that she and her husband occupy. Many people are walking the wide streets, catching a breath of cool air. The weather in Berlin has been just as good as that of the Baltic, and residents treasure summer nights.

The Mosquito raids of the past three nights, and previous sporadic RAF raids, really nuisance strikes, have done comparatively little damage to the sprawling capital. But the German high command has been waiting a long time for massive British raids, and extensive preparations have been made. There are jitters each time the sirens begin to shriek.

Well above London, in Norfolk County, the eight fighter-bombers of the 139th Squadron take off down the runway at Swanton Morley, lift, and soon turn out over the North Sea at low altitude, a tactic designed to keep German radar screens vacant.

Then Group Captain Slee leads his Mosquitoes off toward the neck of Denmark, an area above the German city of Flensburg, always an antiaircraft and fighter hot spot. But there appears to be no Luftwaffe activity over the water this twilight, so the eight planes drum peacefully along toward Whitebait.

Along the east coast of England, almost six hundred RAF bombers manned by English, Scots, Welsh, Australians, New Zealanders, Canadians—even two Americans—are poised to take off with 1,650 tons of bombs and 240 tons of incendiaries. The War Cabinet and Mr. Churchill desire to start many fires.

The first Hydra plane, a Stirling of the 90th Squadron, Air Group 3, thunders down the runway at RAF West Wickham, in Cambridgeshire County. It is 8:28 P.M.—already 9:28 P.M. in Peenemünde and Berlin. The Stirlings, first British four-engined bombers to go into action in the war, are already obsolete, fifteen or twenty m.p.h. slower than the Lancasters and Halifaxes.

Master Bomber Searby is off at 9:50 P.M. from Wyton, in his Lancaster named *William*, going ahead of the Pathfinder squadron so as to arrive early over the target. The other Pathfinders will depart soon, carrying their assortments of varicolored flares and target indicators.

William rumbles along about two hundred feet above the rippled North Sea for two hours, ducking under enemy radar. Then Searby lifts it to one thousand feet to cross over Denmark, sneaking by the night-fighter field on Sylt Island, just below the Danish border.

Night is hooding down and the full moon is rising, putting a silver crust on the ocean as, finally, all the Hydra planes grind north and east.

Slee's eight raiders drop window as they cross Denmark between Flensburg and Esbjerg at 20,000 feet, confusing the German operators below. Dozens of Danish islands, large and small, are below, and the Swedish coast is visible. Malmö, largest city at the tip of Sweden, is lit up beautifully. The Mosquito pilots have not seen a lighted city in a long time.

Sixty miles from the Danish coast, at designated Point A, the main bomber force and the Pathfinders, minus Searby, make rendezvous for the crossing of Denmark and the run over the Baltic and on into target. For the most part, Hydra is on schedule, and the force is intact aside from some twenty aircraft that had to turn back or didn't leave the runway due to engine trouble.

The bombers are at 16,000 feet and the Pathfinders up at 18,000. The roar of the four-engined aircraft fills the moonlit sky. Twenty miles from the Danish shore, clearly outlined, the window strips begin to fall, hobbling radar sets in the air and on the ground. Two bundles drop from each plane, the paper strips shimmering slowly down.

Soon, searchlights stab up and one Pathfinder, flying too far south, is caught in the searching beams above Flensburg and is blown into a ball of fire by ack-ack guns.

The great, dark formation, spread over many miles, roars on. It only takes eleven minutes to cross the neck, the most dangerous part of the flight to this point.

Looking down, the Hydra crews see that the defiant, plucky Danes are acknowledging what's up in the sky. Doors are cracked open, letting light seep out. The RAF is being cheered on silently.

Well ahead of the bombers, the eight Mosquitoes bound for Whitebait head deeper into the Baltic, the pilots marveling at the clarity of the blacked-out islands along the way.

General Dornberger, Dr. von Braun, Ernst Steinhoff, and Hanna Reitsch have separated after dinner, Reitsch driving back to Peenemünde West three miles away. She has that Messerschmitt 163 rocket plane test on the morrow, having flown it before at 625 m.p.h., exceeding the world speed record to that time.

Dr. von Braun is now in his quarters near the administration building; Steinhoff has gone home to his wife and children in the Siedlung; General Dornberger has gone to his apartment in visitors' quarters, which he uses when at the center. Much of his time is now spent in Berlin.

Peenemünde is totally blacked out, yet much of it is visible in the silver light. The big buildings cast oblong shadows.

At High Wycombe, Bomber Harris has retired for the night but knows he'll be awakened when the first radio reports of Hydra reach headquarters. At RAF Wyton, home of Searby's squadron, Duncan Sandys is wide awake and will stay that way until the Master Bomber returns, if he does.

Churchill is in Canada for meetings with President Roosevelt, staying at The Citadel of Quebec, overlooking the St. Lawrence River. He's very much aware that the raid is taking place this night.

About eleven Peenemünde time, in a position west of the ancient seaport city of Rostock, Group Captain Slee turns his eight aircraft due south and heads them directly for Whitebait. Rostock is eighty miles west of Peene-münde, but radar warns all area commands even though these high-flying raiders seem to be following the same pattern as the three nights preceding. Berlin is warned, of course.

At 11:25, sirens begin to wail at the rocket center, Karlshagen, Zinnowitz, and Wolgast, awakening most of those already asleep. The whole area is bathed in moon-light, but no planes are visible in the sky, though warn-ings wail on for a few minutes.

Some residents enter bunkers; many do not. Outside the shelter opposite Haus 4, von Braun's office, no more than ten people gaze upward; no more than ten have gone down into the shelter.

General Dornberger, preparing to go to bed, calls the duty officer and is told, "Allied formations are over the Baltic." He asks for their heading.

"Not yet known, sir," is the answer.

Dornberger goes to bed, believing it is another nui-sance strike at Berlin; nonetheless, he worries about the safety of his wife in their apartment there.

Ack-ack gunners on the roofs of the buildings, their gun barrels poking through camouflage strips, and those at heavier ground batteries stand by, as does the *Undine*. Russian POWs and the elderly home guards manning the smoke machines await orders to make smoke.

Still at high altitude, the Mosquitoes drive on to Whitebait, paying no attention to Peenemünde or Ros-tock. The German countryside is dark, and thus far no radar-equipped night fighters have come out of their de-fensive "boxes" to engage in combat.

This raid on Berlin is purely a deception move, of course, and Bomber Harris couldn't really care less how much damage the Mosquitoes accomplish. Each carries three 500-pound bombs and a target indicator, the latter to persuade the Germans that heavy bombers are on the way.

Slee's planes arrive on the outskirts of the city just before midnight, but many, if not most, of the four million Berliners are already in the air-raid shelters, having obediently answered the full alarm. Ack-ack batteries have been waiting for almost an hour, as have some of the night fighters, summoned from as far away as France.

Early radio warnings had said, "Heavy bombers massing over the Baltic . . ."

At 12:31 A.M., monitoring British radio operators in London hear the fighter controller at the Luftwaffe 12th Air Corps repeating, "All night fighters to Berlin, all night fighters to Berlin . . ."

Bomber Command's chess game has worked!

Junkers 88s, Dornier 217s, and Messerschmitt 110s zoom up from fields in France, Holland, Belgium, and Denmark, as well as interior Germany.

A furious barrage of ack-ack opens up as the individual Mosquitoes, flying at different altitudes and on different courses, streak across the great city. Searchlight beams are reaching everywhere for the phantom planes, and the night fighters take to the sky. Not only are some caught in the bursting flak, there is one midair collision. By this time, 150 German night fighters are converging on the capital.

The 500-pounders drop from the Mosquitoes and the target indicators go down, causing wilder confusion on the ground. Ack-ack has never been so heavy over jittery Berlin. In fact, there are more casualties from shrapnel than from the British bombs.

One Mosquito is shot down by a Messerschmitt 110, but seven of them, including Group Captain Slee's, head abruptly west at 12:40, fleeing back for Swanton Morley, job well done.

Over the Baltic, the heavy bombers of Hydra are a hundred miles from Peenemünde and closing.

14. My Poor Peenemünde

Some of the bombers arrive early and now circle in metallic light over the Baltic, north of target, awaiting the others. The first Pathfinder flares are planned for drop at 1:11 A.M. Usedom time, but few military operations are ever precisely on schedule. On final approach, strung out for miles, the aircraft are like oncoming black vultures, blue-red licks of exhaust gushing out from the four engines.

Master Bomber Searby is first to fly over Peenemünde in *William*. The shoreline, blacked-out buildings, electric railway tracks, athletic field, and housing area are all remarkably clear. Before Searby ends his first pass, the sirens are wailing below, smoke generators start to puff, and the breeze begins to push the gray veils northwestward.

At about six thousand feet, Searby swings to the left and goes out over the sea, switching on his radio to contact the Pathfinders and the main force. Operation Hydra is about to begin. Fortunately for all, most of the German night fighters are still milling about Berlin or flying toward it, German Fighter Command still believing the attack will be against the capital.

The Pathfinder plan is to mark the route to target by dropping the first "red fire spots" on nearby tiny Rügen Island, seven miles from target, aiming them blindly by radar from high altitude. In effect, the line of burning red spots will be an arrow pointing toward Usedom and target, similar to road flares. Then timing and visual marking with varicolored flares will aid successive waves of bombers to hit the three primary target areas, beginning with the housing estates.

At nine minutes, thirty-six seconds past one A.M., the first fire spots drop from a high-flying Lancaster over the northwest tip of Usedom, not Rügen as planned, exploding at 3,000 feet, then dropping to earth to burn furiously. This late drop automatically sets up an error, and the innocent POW barracks, well beyond the Siedlung, are in for terrible and unplanned punishment.

Over the next five minutes, more fire spots drop, along with red, green, yellow, and white flares, as the visual markers go down. At last, ack-ack batteries begin firing, throwing flak up to 15,000 feet. Searchlights begin waving back and forth, seeking out bombers, lighting them up for the ground gunners.

Outside, looking at the sky filled with colors, Dornberger stands transfixed for a moment. Later, he said, "The scene that met my gaze had a sinister and appealing beauty of its own."

With Searby making another coordinating run over targets, calmly directing marking traffic, the initial attack begins at 1:15 A.M. with a total of 211 bombers, plus Pathfinders, making runs on the housing estates but hitting as far southeast as poor Trassenheide with its population of prisoners.

As bombs begin to fall, Dornberger, von Braun, and other occupants of the bachelors' and visitors' quarters move quickly to the large shelter in front of Haus 4, safest bunker on the island. Almost three hundred people are already in the long room.

Added to the smoke and flares are now the blinding flashes of bombs that weigh up to two tons. To those huddling in makeshift and sand-trench shelters, or in the housing estates' basements, it seems that the earth is heaving. Eardrums burst. Some shelters collapse. To the Poles, Ukranians, and other people locked up in the forty-seven barracks at Trassenheide, a deafening, fiery storm has swept over them. Screaming, burning men try to claw out. Many guards have fled the fire and destruction, leaving prisoners to die.

Bombs keep falling on the POW camp and the Siedlung for almost fifteen minutes until both are roaring masses of flames. The pinewoods are on fire as well.

At the urging of Walter Riedel, who lives next door, Dr. Thiel, his wife, and four children had fled to a slit trench on Hindenburgstrasse. A bomb soon makes a direct hit on it and all perish. Riedel and his own family survive in a basement.

Bombs are falling to water's edge in front of the single-women's residences, and the Kameradschaftsheim, which echoed to song the previous evening, is now blazing.

Beach sand is blowing five or six hundred feet into the air, and people are wading out into the water, hoping to escape; some go in the opposite direction, fleeing into the woods.

Finally, the antiaircraft batteries begin to find targets. One bomber is burning, sloping down toward the sea in a final dive. Airmen jump out and parachutes pop. Another bomber simply disappears in an orange-red ball as heavy guns reach it.

By now, it is realized that the Mosquitoes over Berlin had been nothing more than bait to attract German night fighters. A few of the fighters have been shot down by friendly ack-ack fire; several have even attacked each other; fuel is running low, and the runways at Brandenburg Field are soon a mess. Some thirty defenders of Berlin have crash-landed or collided with others on landing. However, another thirty, with ample fuel aboard, wheel around and head for Peenemünde, twenty minutes away.

In that direction, there is a dull red oval on the horizon. Albert Speer, standing in a Berlin flak tower, sees the red glow and immediately guesses that the Usedom center is under attack.

Master Bomber Searby is making another run over the

dense smoke and mushrooms of fire, still calmly giving orders and advice, sounding as if he were routing double-decker buses around Trafalgar Square.

Then the attack is shifted by new Pathfinder markers to the second target area, Werke Süd, the rocket assembly buildings. Even if the pilots had known about the terrified concentration camp boarders living in the lower part of the south building, bombs would still fall. More than two hundred aircraft go after the assembly halls and smaller surrounding buildings. Four hundred tons will drop in this area.

As the earth shakes and dust falls in the bunker near Haus 4, Dornberger, fully dressed in his uniform and leather coat, is handed a pair of boots and leaves the shelter with von Braun to direct fire fighting. The brigades are spreading throughout the area to battle flames in the work areas, leaving housing to burn.

At last, the Messerschmitts and Dorniers, foiled over Berlin, begin to arrive about 1:40 A.M., aching for battle. One quickly sends a Lancaster down, engulfed in flames.

To those in the bombers, drumming in across target at altitudes of 4,000 feet—dangerously low—the whole of Usedom seems to be burning. Air is turbulent, not only from heat but from the upward blast of the two-ton "Tall Boy" blockbusters.

The attack against the rocket assembly plants lasts for about eleven minutes; then the surviving Lancasters of Group One, some of them crossing the target area several times, turn and begin to toil back to England, knowing that further attack from night fighters is probable.

Searby's final excursion over the smoking, burning maelstrom begins about 1:48 A.M. So far, he's led a charmed life, making the run over target six times, ack-ack reaching for him each time. He advises the new arrivals, "Bomb the greens" (the green flares dropped by the Pathfinders), and heads for home.

Groups Five and Six are paying heavily for earlier deception of the night fighters. Special Luftwaffe Wild

Boar units are chopping up the bombers, skidding around, shooting them down as quickly as they can line up on a target.

Said one pilot later, "All over the sky, RAF planes were coming down in flaming infernos."

Final bombs are dropped at 2:07 A.M. and Hydra is over. The raid has lasted almost an hour.

As all-clear signals whine over stricken Peenemünde, ambulances begin to roll. The shell-shocked inhabitants emerge from bunkers, basements, and slit trenches or stagger out of the woods, all stunned by what they see. Devastation. Fires everywhere. Bodies everywhere, some charred beyond recognition.

General Dornberger, narrowly escaping being trapped in his burning apartment while trying to rescue personal effects, says, "My poor, poor Peenemünde." He's in tears.

Blond hair turned white with shelter dust, von Braun runs with his secretary to rescue secret documents out of the second floor of the fiercely burning administration building. Soon, they are tossing papers and files out of windows.

Fires are still burning as dawn breaks, but it will be hours, even days, before the full extent of damages can be determined.

At Wyton RAF base, not long after Group Commander Searby lands safely, Duncan Sandys is able to call Churchill in Quebec. Though Searby refuses to commit himself as to damage until he sees aerial photos, Sandys believes that he has heard enough to tell the prime minister, "Operation Hydra has been a success."

15. Assessment

Dornberger is certain that the British will return, and at about 11:00 A.M., air-raid sirens howl again as a lone plane from the 540th Squadron snaps pictures of the still-smoking burning target area. By late afternoon, the film is in processing tanks.

On Usedom, it is a time of shock, anger, sorrow, and work. The last of the fires are extinguished; bodies and parts of bodies are being collected. Hundreds died in the Trassenheide camp, more than a hundred in the housing estates and dormitory area. But luck was with the key scientific staff. The British did not accomplish a primary goal—to kill the main rocket team. Pale, bespectacled Dr. Thiel, the engine expert, is dead; Dr. Erich Walther, chief maintenance engineer at Werke Süd is dead. But hundreds of scientists, engineers, and technicians are very much alive.

Dornberger and von Braun fly over the area to assess damage, and Speer arrives from Berlin to make a first-hand survey. He confers briefly with the weary, disheveled Dornberger, snaps some pictures to show Hitler, and then departs.

By early afternoon, it is known that the greatest damage was done to Trassenheide and the housing estates. Ninety percent destroyed. The two rocket assembly buildings at Werke Süd were hit and a few rockets destroyed or damaged, but both structures will be easy to repair. The scientific section has suffered, particularly the administration building, but the prized wind tunnel and Steinhoff's crucial Measurement House, the telemetry building, aren't even pocked. Test stands are whole; the power plant is undamaged; the liquid-oxygen plant is intact.

"Contrary to first impressions, the damage is small," Dornberger reports to superiors.

He decides to leave Peenemünde much as it looks now—cratered, bombed out, burnt out, useless. In fact, Dornberger orders that burnt timbers be placed across the roof of Haus 4. Photo-recco planes are certain to visit frequently, and Dornberger wants an abandoned look from the air.

A few days go by before a final count of casualties is completed. After the horrors of Trassenheide and the housing estates are picked over, it is estimated that 732 people have died in the attack, of whom only 120 were German. Dornberger considers himself lucky.

Speer visits Hitler on August 19, giving him a fuller account of the damage but also guessing that the program won't lose more than six weeks because of the raid. But Dornberger and von Braun believe that the rocket center will be hit again. Another decision they make is to have the wind tunnel dismantled and moved to the Bavarian mountains. An overland testing range will have to be established as well. Though Hydra has not been successful, Peenemünde will never be the same.

By this time, seventy-two hours after the raid, Bomber Command at High Wycombe also has estimates on the British cost. Forty bombers have not returned and are listed as missing. Added to those are two Mosquitoes of the Berlin feint, one having crash-landed on return. Almost three hundred pilots and crewmen are either dead or missing. The price is high.

The Luftwaffe has also counted its losses: From all the activity—Berlin, Peenemünde, and elsewhere—it appears that twelve night fighters have been lost in combat or from ack-ack fire, another fourteen lost or severely damaged in ground accidents.

Mass graves are dug along the twisted railway tracks, and on Saturday, August 21, another warm and sunny day on Usedom, mass funeral services are held, with a Lutheran minister and a Catholic priest talking of the hardships and sacrifices of war. The Zinnowitz Promenade Concert Band plays funeral dirges, and then cleanup work resumes.

Next morning, Heinrich Himmler arrives at Wolf's Lair to see Hitler. The SS chief believes that the time is right for a push of the A-4 program elsewhere than on Usedom. He offers to speed rocket production by providing more concentration camp labor coupled with technical assists from his own corps.

After an all-day and part-of-the-night meeting with the Führer and Speer, decisions are made to use Himmler's SS training camp area near Blizna, Poland, for a new test range and to speed up construction of the huge underground assembly plant in the mountains of central Germany. The officer that Himmler has in mind to expedite everything is none other than his own brigadier general, Dr. Hans Kammler, SS engineer.

Hitler approves of the plan and especially of Dr. Kammler, the brown-eyed, handsome forty-two-year-old designer of gas chambers and other works, a man with a quick wit and winning personality.

General Dornberger is startled and alarmed by this choice of Kammler and is frightened by the speed with which Himmler has moved into the rocket program. He can do nothing about either circumstance.

Himmler's training camp at Blizna, 170 miles south of Warsaw, is in thick woods of pine, fir, and oak. Kammler immediately begins construction of barracks and living quarters for officers. Railroad tracks are laid and double barbed-wire fences soon enclose the area.

Himmler also proposes that the Peenemünde development works, von Braun's main activity, be moved to a large cave blasted out of an Austrian mountain.

No day seems to go by without a turn of events that involves Heinrich Himmler one way or another. With about six thousand of Himmler's slave laborers doing the chores, concrete is being poured this late August for the huge storage and rocket-firing bunker in France, across from England's white cliffs of Dover. This is the installation that contains almost as much concrete as Boulder Dam.

Much of the mixture is still soft and moist on August 27 when Flying Fortresses from the U.S. Eighth Air Force drop low-level loads on it. The French countryside is splattered for a quarter mile, and Kraftwerke Nordwest is soon abandoned. There is glee in London. Civil engineers had been viewing photos of the construction for weeks and had finally said, "Hit it tomorrow!"

After hearing reports of the "wet concrete" assault, an enraged Hitler demands another attempt at permanently housing the rockets on the French coast. Soon, engineers propose a "million-ton dome of solid concrete" under which will be mined a hundred-foot-deep cavern with tunnels projecting like spokes of a wheel. The A-4 will roll along a tunnel, foot-thick bombproof steel doors will spring open, and the rocket will be launched from this new installation near Watten.

It may all sound like science fiction, but the drawing boards of the Todt Organization, the construction supervisors, begin to indicate otherwise.

16. Bodilsker Church

The island of Bornholm, most easterly of Denmark's five hundred islands, sits in the Baltic seventy miles north of Usedom, below Sweden. Nazi troops had occupied it three years ago, and the proud, tough Bornholmers have been resisting in every possible way. One way is to "accidentally" knock down an enemy pedestrian with a bike, apologize profusely, then repeat the same accident with another soldier a mile or two up the lane.

At five minutes past one P.M., Sunday, August 23, the police sergeant at Nexo, a village on the east coast of Bornholm, receives a call reporting that an "aircraft has crashed about two kilometers from Bodilsker church." The sergeant immediately phones Danish police headquarters in Rønne, the capital, across on the other side of the island. In turn, the German army commander is notified.

Witnesses living near the church tell Sergeant Pederson that the aircraft came in low, with a "whistling sound," before dropping into the turnip field.

About an hour later, Lieutenant Commander Hasagar Christiansen, ranking officer of the Danish navy on the island, arrives at the crash site along with the chief of police from Rønne. What they see is not a conventional aircraft! There is no cockpit, much less a pilot. No propellers. Puzzled, Christiansen assumes it is some type of remote-controlled "training bomb" and quickly photographs it.

Ten minutes later, a pair of German officers arrive. They, too, are puzzled. Soon, the wreckage of the apparatus is loaded into a large truck and sent on to German army headquarters in Rønne.

When asked by one of the officers if he photographed the wreckage, Christiansen says emphatically that he did not. Never would he do such a thing!

Next day, his photographs, plus a report and sketch, are headed out of Danish territory. Three different sets, bound eventually for London, leave Bornholm and find their way to three different underground messengers.

One messenger is a lowly deckhand on the ferry that runs from Elsinore, the castle town of *Hamlet* fame, over to Helsingborg, in Sweden. How it happens is never discovered, but the Danish sailor is caught with one of Christiansen's sets. He is soon executed.

Christiansen is also arrested and charged with espionage. Tortured by the Gestapo, he remembers little of the next six weeks. Finally he is spirited out of a hospital by Danish underground members and transferred to safety in Sweden.

Two sets of the photos make it to England, and one goes to the desk of Dr. Jones. Studying the photos and Christiansen's report of what the Bornholmers heard before the object crashed, Jones is not at all certain what is in front of him. The report indicates a length of "about four meters," or thirteen feet, and Jones thinks the wreckage might be that of a glider bomb currently being used against British ships in the Mediterranean.

Whatever it is, chances are good that it came from Peenemünde, mistakenly landing on Bornholm.

Two other intelligence reports come in at about the same time. One says that a pilotless aircraft is being tested at Peenemünde; the other, from a French agent, declares that rocket attacks on London will begin in October and that a colonel named Wachtel is training men to launch missiles. The information is correct.

17. Can England Be Defended?

On September 21, Churchill addresses the House of Commons, saying, in part: "Speeches of the German leaders contain mysterious allusions to new methods and new weapons which will be tried against us. It would, of course, be natural for the enemy to spread such rumors in order to encourage his own people. But there is probably more to it than that."

Rumors? Allied intelligence has a wild, bumper crop of them: Missiles containing huge tanks of poison gas are going to be fired on London; London will be hit with containers of liquid "red death," a few drops of which will kill instantly and gruesomely; those big concrete monstrosities at Watten and Wizernes, on the French coast, are actually gigantic refrigerators for manufacturing icebergs in the English Channel or for dropping clouds of ice over England, knocking down Allied aircraft.

Dr. Jones prefers to believe only in the rocket threat. Though there is overwhelming evidence from aerial photos and members of the underground, no absolute information has yet been developed as to exact type, range, and explosive power of either the long-range rockets or the flying bombs. Despite all his good detective work, Dr. Jones has no answer to Churchill's basic question: Can England be defended against these weapons?

A few days later, he advises Churchill, "Although Hitler would press the rockets into service at the earliest possible moment, that moment is probably months ahead.''

Churchill then advises President Roosevelt, ''I ought to let you know that during the last six months evidence has continued to accumulate that the Germans are planning an attack on England, particularly London, by means of very long-range rockets which conceivably weigh sixty tons and carry an explosive charge of ten to twenty tons.''

Few days go by that the prime minister does not expertly needle his son-in-law Duncan Sandys, Lord Cherwell, Dr. Jones, the air minister, or anyone else who might possibly have some answers. There is a continuing argument among the officials as to size, range, and amount of explosives.

News of enemy missile research does not really surprise U.S. scientists and military officers involved in new weapons development. But German atomic capability tied to rocket development makes for great uneasiness, and Major General Leslie Groves, head of the Manhattan Project, the American atom bomb project, soon organizes the ALSOS Mission, a scientific intelligence operation that will follow behind invasion forces to capture enemy scientists and equipment such as may be in use at Peenemünde.

In late September, Heinrich Himmler visits the new Polish overland firing range at Blizna. Hans Kammler also pays a visit. Dornberger resents his presence, but Dr. Kammler is firmly in charge of all construction concerning the A-4 and has legitimate business at Blizna.

As laid out, the impact point will be almost two hundred miles away to the northeast, in the Pripet marshes. While firing over the Baltic has been ideal for safety, the rocket makers now need to observe personally the performance of the A-4 just before impact, and the impact itself. Some of the rockets have broken up or exploded prior to reaching target or misbehaved in other ways. Eyewitnessing is best. Blizna will also serve to train troops to launch the missile.

In addition to the Pripet marshes, there is another impact area, 150 miles away—the entire village of Sarnaki, though the residents haven't been informed. There is no known case in the history of war where an entire inhabited town has been used for target practice.

Meanwhile, Dr. Kammler's priority work goes on beneath Kohnstein Mountain. The parallel mile-and-a-quarter main tunnels, linked by forty-six connecting tunnels and with galleries at appropriate places, will house all of the machinery developed at Peenemünde to produce both the A-4 and the flying bomb. Production will resemble a Detroit assembly line—slowly traveling chassis to which parts are added until the completed missiles emerge. Nineteen of the tunnels will be used for jet-engine assembly.

The weather is bitterly cold in the Blizna area on November 5 as the first rocket is fired in the direction of snow-covered Pripet. The rumbling A-4 thaws the ground around the launch table but travels no more than two miles.

The weather over most of Europe is miserable this wintry month, as usual, and although Dr. Jones has requested the 540th Squadron to return over Peenemünde, no mission can be flown. The Baltic is socked in almost solidly.

As of the end of this first week of November, British and USAAF photo-reconnaissance planes have flown more than three thousand missions over the French, Belgian, and Dutch coasts, about fifty to Peenemünde and surrounding areas. A million and a quarter prints have been made of these photos, all in search of *wunder* weapon evidence. Since early September, pilots have had standing orders to seek out and photograph likely launch sites for a flying bomb, a contraption or device, they are told, that might have short wings and look like a tiny aircraft.

Okay, say the pilots, but what will be the appearance of the launch site itself? No one knows, not even Dr. Jones.

Yet some rather interesting features have shown up in some of the hundreds of thousands of aerial photos of the north coast areas of France. Eyes have stared at them until bleariness sets in. So far, twenty-six of these strange installations have been spotted. For lack of other identification, they have been designated "ski" buildings.

Made of concrete, they are shaped like skis, and are estimated to be about 270 feet in length. Windowless, they appear to have thick walls. The entrance to each "ski" is estimated to be twenty-two feet wide, which might or might not accommodate a large rocket with its fins folded. Yet it seems to the analysts, Jones included, that it would be rather difficult to maneuver a missile the size of those seen in Peenemünde in and out of the "ski" doors. No giant cranes to lift the missiles are visible.

Nearby is a rectangular building with large doors on either end. Paths lead from this building to the ski-shaped building. Then there is what appears to be a long, narrow, concrete ramp. Paths lead there, too.

On examination of a number of photos, it is noted that the ramps all point in one direction: *London!*

On November 28, weathermen indicate a possible break in the clouds over the Baltic shore, and Squadron Leader John Merifield takes off in his Mosquito for the western Baltic. The forecasters were correct. Merifield finds some holes in the clouds over Usedom and cameras click.

Though most training is now in East Prussia, there is considerable agitation down in little Zempin, where part of Colonel Max Wachtel's 155 W Regiment is functioning. The last time the British pinpointed a target on this stretch of island, tons of blockbusters fell out of the sky.

Merifield's photos are processed that night, and to everyone's dismay they are of very poor quality. Yet there are three long, inclined ramps clearly visible on the

Zempin shore, and all of them look exactly like the London-aimed ramps that are apparent near the "ski" buildings on the French coast.

At home in Richmond, bedded down with a sore throat and flu, Dr. Jones soon examines the Zempin prints, comparing them with the photos from France. There's no doubt in his mind that the ramps are identical in both places and are of the type that will shortly be used to launch some sort of flying bomb.

At dreary Medmenham, in the chilly, bulky gray mansion of Danesfield, Flight Officer Constance Babington-Smith had already restudied all of the thousands of Peenemünde photos taken prior to Hydra. On one, she'd discovered a previously unseen, perhaps "not significant," type of aircraft. Small. Wingspan of about twenty feet. She'd been troubled by it at the time, unable to draw any worthwhile conclusion.

Now she closely examines the Zempin photos. On the center ramp, she spots a "tiny, cruciform shape, set exactly in the lower end of the inclined rails, a midget aircraft actually in position for launching." It has no cockpit and a wingspan of nineteen feet, meaning it could easily go through the "ski" entrance. This likely means that the "ski" building is a hangar. At any rate, this midget aircraft is the same as the perhaps "not significant" one she'd seen earlier.

As of this moment, the British have finally discovered the Fi 103, or FZG 76, or Vengeance 1—the V-1, as the world will soon know it.

In measured steps, Flight Officer Babington-Smith walks down the gloomy corridor to her superior's office.

Operation Bodyline, the Sandys investigation of German secret weapons, now becomes Crossbow, headed by Winston Churchill himself. One of Churchill's first directives is to destroy all known "ski" sites. Large-scale bombing raids by the U.S. Eighth Air Force begin a few days before Christmas with Flying Fortresses dropping 1,700 tons of bombs.

So apprehensive are the members of the War Cabinet, especially Churchill, that British intelligence is given the improbable "James Bond" assignment of kidnapping one of the Peenemünde scientists with the idea of persuading him to talk, one way or another. Though this plot is never carried out, it is discussed in all seriousness.

Behind much of the apprehension is an operation coded Overlord, the invasion of Europe under Supreme Allied Commander General Dwight D. Eisenhower. Overlord is scheduled for summer and there is fear that an all-out enemy rocket and flying bomb attack could postpone the invasion, particularly if it is directed at the ports needed for loading and handling of millions of tons of war supplies.

More and more "ski" sites are discovered, and there is fear that usual bombing techniques will not work, that the Germans will win in the race against time.

On January 25, General Henry "Hap" Arnold, chief of the U.S. Army Air Forces, calls the commanding officer of Eglin Field, Florida, to outline the problem. He wants the "ski" sites reproduced in the barren 800,000 acres of Eglin's proving ranges. "I want to make simulated attacks with a new weapon. I want the job done in *days,* not weeks. It will take a hell of a lot of concrete. . . . give it *first priority . . .*"

Photos and descriptions of the sites are flown to Eglin that day, and General Gardner goes to work duplicating them in a section of the base far from public view. Thousands of civilian employees and airmen work around the clock, having no idea of the purpose of the odd-looking concrete, steel, and wooden buildings.

After camouflage is added, even antiaircraft batteries, the sites are bombed with every weapon in the USAAF arsenal, the pilots having no idea why they are attacking these funny-looking structures in the remote pinewoods of the Florida panhandle. Some are hit before the concrete even sets.

General Gardner reports each day's results to Hap

Arnold, and it is finally decided that the best method of destroying the launch sites is to go in at low level and conduct precision raids with heavy bombs. This is also the most dangerous way to do the job.

18. Himmler Again

On New Year's Day, 1944, the first three A-4s emerge from the exit tunnel of Mittelwerke, now employing about ten thousand slave laborers and convicts. Some never see daylight. Those from the concentration camp at Nordhausen are marched to Mittelwerke at four o'clock each morning; those at Camp Dora, connected to the underground factory, simply march through a tunnel. Within a month's time, the factory will be ready to start full mass production of both the rocket and the flying bomb.

Placed nose to nose on railroad cars, two to every three cars, and covered with tarpaulins, the first few rockets head for Wolgast under heavy guard. No papers indicate the nature of this cargo aside from its destination, and SS guards are ordered to stay away from the tarps. Other special trains will soon carry missiles to the range in Poland as well. In both Peenemünde and Blizna, these factory-produced rockets will be tested for reliability.

Toward the end of January, von Braun flies to Mittelwerke to review procedures and visit with his younger brother, Magnus, who is in charge of the gyroscope assembly. Though von Braun is accustomed to imaginative projects, he is astonished at General Dr. Kammler's tunneling plans, over and above the astonishing labyrinth for missile production. Kammler has created caverns for an underground oil refinery, jet-engine manufacture, and solid-fuel missiles.

Von Braun flies on to Blizna to begin evaluating the A-4s on the new overland range. Production models tested thus far at Peenemünde have not performed very well, and he already knows the basic reason—the program has been pushed along too fast. Yet the current pressures from Wolf's Lair and Berlin demand performance, not excuses.

In early February, observing in the Pripet marsh impact area, von Braun leaves the safety bunker, believing that the day's testing is over, and suddenly finds himself in the open with a missile spearing down. Flattening his body, he survives the explosion three hundred feet away.

But the danger in the Polish marsh is not as great, in many ways, as the danger that lies in the East Prussian woods, now headquarters of the SS Reichsführer. The night von Braun returns to Peenemünde he is summoned by Himmler.

The next day, having no idea why the SS chief wants to see him, von Braun flies to East Prussia. After pleasantries are exchanged, Himmler says, "I have been informed that you're having problems with the A-4."

"Nothing that we can't solve in time," von Braun replies.

"Time is running out," says Himmler. "I hope you realize that your A-4 rocket has ceased to be a toy and that the whole German people eagerly await the mystery weapon."

"I'm aware of that, Reichsführer," von Braun replies.

"Why not join my staff? Surely you know that no one has such ready access to the Führer, and I promise you vastly more effective programming than those hidebound generals can give you. The Führer is losing confidence in the army."

"Reichsführer, I couldn't ask for a better chief than General Dornberger. Such delays as we're experiencing are due to technical troubles, not red tape. . . ."

A few minutes later, Dr. von Braun is politely dismissed; Himmler is still cordial and smiling as the scientist leaves the heavily camouflaged, lavishly furnished railway car. But the conversation is unnerving and occupies von Braun's mind as he takes off from Rastenburg for the flight back to Usedom.

For the most part, von Braun has been working seven days a week since the beginning of the war, but he does feel the need to relax now and then. Along with Klaus Riedel and Dr. Helmuth Grottrup, assistant chief of telemetry, he attends a private party in Zinnowitz on the first Sunday in March. A number of scientists and engineers from the center are also present, as are a few townspeople.

Drinks are served, food is laid out, and after a while von Braun, Riedel, and Grottrup talk at length about the future and space travel. The war is too painful, possibly too dangerous, to discuss. Talking about space travel with friends is something von Braun has done since he first met Willy Ley in 1929. The afternoon and evening are most enjoyable.

A week later, von Braun is arrested by Gestapo agents in his quarters at 3:00 A.M. and charged with sabotage of the A-4 program. After two weeks in prison at Stettin, he is hauled to court on fake charges.

Riedel and Grottrup are also taken into custody, charged with the same crimes. Himmler obviously has spies in the research center and surrounding towns. A woman dentist who attended the party and overheard von Braun is responsible for the arrests.

Specifically, von Braun is charged with being more interested in rocket development for future space flight than in weapons development for the war. He's certainly guilty of that, but so are most of the key scientists at Peenemünde. He is also charged with planning an escape to England with rocket secrets, a charge he denies as ridiculous.

Both General Dornberger and von Braun believe that Dr. Kammler is actually responsible for the arrests. The SS engineer had been making disparaging remarks about von Braun for several months, and the refusal to join Himmler's "team" simply brought the matter to a head.

Behind scenes, Dornberger works furiously, involving Albert Speer and others in an effort to free the trio. He finally makes it known at Wolf's Lair that the rocket program will cease if von Braun stays in jail or is executed. All three men are released, but Himmler is not finished with personal designs on rocket making.

19. The Bug River "Fish"

On a foggy dawn this month of March, a Polish underground member known to the British as Makary crawls up to the rail line that leads into the Blizna installation simply to take a look around. He sees an object wrapped in a wet tarpaulin occupying two flat cars that are heavily guarded by SS troops. Judging it to be a "monstrous torpedo," Makary slithers back into the woods. About a week later his report reaches Dr. Jones.

There has been intelligence information dating back to 1941 of an SS artillery range near Blizna, and just before Makary's message filters in, there is a separate sketchy underground account of "concrete structures, barbed-wire fences, aerial torpedoes being fired . . ."

To that time, Jones had concluded that Blizna was probably a practice range for flying bombs. However, an object that occupies two flat cars is definitely not a flying bomb. Early in the war England had broken Germany's Enigma code and was now privy to messages sent by Enigma. One recent decoded message spoke of a crater that had been found at Sidlice, 160 miles northeast of Blizna. No German flying bomb had that range, in Jones's opinion. He hazarded a guess that the Sidlice crater was made by a long-range rocket, that Blizna was now an operating launching site.

It is one thousand miles to Blizna from Oxfordshire, the nearest RAF photoreconnaissance base, and even the staunch Mosquito, with its extra fuel tanks, cannot make that round trip in one haul. But Jones desperately wants Blizna covered and puts in an urgent request for same.

Not until April 15, after Allied armies begin fighting their way up the Italian "boot," does a Blizna flight become possible. A PRU base is established at San Severo, over toward the Adriatic Sea, and a Mosquito photo plane takes to the air for the six-hundred-mile flight deep into Poland.

Jones is disappointed when the photos reveal little more than a "large clearing in the woods and some heavily camouflaged buildings." But he does spot a flying bomb ramp and remains convinced that sooner or later he'll find a rocket. More coverage of Blizna is requested.

Another flight from San Severo returns over the Blizna woods on May 5, and this time the Medmenham interpreters discover a single rocket out in the open. Proof enough, in Jones's opinion.

Fifteen days later there is more proof as an A-4 plunges into the Bug River near the village of Sarnaki. Members of the underground, several from Sarnaki, reach the river before motorized SS personnel arrive.

The armed missile is in shallow water, fins sticking out, and the Poles push it deeper into the mud and then drive cattle into the water, stirring it up. When the SS searchers arrive, asking if anyone has seen a rocket, the Poles play dumb.

"We are just minding our cattle," they say.

However, that night a message starts on its way to London: *We have a rocket!*

Three days later, after the Germans stop hunting, the missile is removed from the river bottom by sheer strength, not a crane, and is transported to a barn in the village of Holoczyce-Kolonia, outside the immediate range area.

The British inform the Poles that they don't need the entire rocket, just vital parts plus accurate, detailed drawings and measurements. Scientists from Warsaw headed by young Anton Kocjan, whose specialty is aerodynamics, begin that job. It cannot be accomplished overnight.

20. Diver

Allied Crossbow raids on the French coast "ski" sites have continued, costing the lives of 771 airmen and 154 bombers, but Colonel Wachtel has not been seriously delayed in his push to begin action with 155 W Regiment. In this June of 1944, he has many units ready to operate although only three thousand of the buzz bombs are available for mass attack. Though he'd like to delay, Hitler has ordered bombardment to start by mid-month.

Delays and desires become academic June 6, D-day, when the Allies move across the English Channel in Overlord, invading Normandy. The same evening, Wachtel receives the code word *Junk-Room* from Berlin, a signal to commence operations six days hence. Units of 155 W begin moving equipment to designated launch sites. Trains from Nordhausen are unloaded. The pulse-jet flying bombs manufactured in Mittelwerke begin their next-to-final journey.

The new and simple method of launch is from a 150-foot-long catapult that can be swiftly erected in the woods, supported by steel girders and logs. The "ski" site operation is already obsolete. A steam piston operated by chemicals sends the flying bomb, its pulse jet puffing away, up the catapult. After going off the ramp at about 150 m.p.h., it picks up speed to about 400, automatic pilot pointing it toward England.

While the world's attention is focused on the fierce fighting along Normandy's beaches, Wachtel's engi-

neers work feverishly to ready the attack by June 12.
Many things go wrong at all the sites and Wachtel pleads
for more time. His requests are promptly denied. Bombardment will divert Allied aircraft away from Normandy, Hitler decrees.

At Medmenham, it is noted that there have been
changes within the last six days at nine of the sixty-six
known, and probably operational, "ski" sites. What is
not known is that the Germans no longer need those sites
as the new method requires only trucks and portable cata-
pults.

Diver will be the British code word for flying bombs,
according to a Defence Secret Instruction, and should be
passed immediately if one is sighted. However, most civilians in England have never heard of a flying bomb,
and it is likely 98 percent of all military personnel are ig-
norant of the code word.

Besides, the excitement of Overlord and the European
invasion overshadows any thoughts of air attack by conventional weapons or otherwise. By late afternoon June
12, the Allies have driven twelve miles into France and
are threatening to break through along the entire Nazi
front. The war-weary British people stay by radios
awaiting good news.

Not long after midnight, German big guns across from
Dover send eight shells into Maidstone, several miles inland. Then shells drop on Folkestone, also on the Dover
Straits. The whistling hot steel stops abruptly at 4:00
A.M. A few minutes later an auxiliary coastguardsman on
the harbor jetty at Folkestone logs the approach of "two
aircraft with lighted cockpits." They make a "strange
noise, like a two-stroke motor-bike engine headed up-
hill."

The coastguardsman has never heard of flying bombs,
nor the code word *Diver*.

At 4:18 A.M., the first Fi 103 hits near Gravesend,
twenty miles short of its target, the famed Tower Bridge
over the Thames. A moment later, another robot bomb

explodes at Cuckfield; a third hits a railway bridge at Bethnal Green, killing six people; a fourth drops on Seven Oaks.

The terror-weapon campaign has finally begun, and one man taking great pleasure is Dr. Josef Goebbels, Nazi minister of propaganda. He is shown color films of the next step, the A-4, beginning with its manufacture in the limestone tunnels beneath Mount Kohnstein, ending with a dozen missiles being launched.

He officially names the flying bomb *Vergeltungswaffe*, Vengeance 1, and the A-4, Vengeance 2.

Radio Berlin announces to the world that the German *wunder* weapons will soon bring England to its knees.

While debris is being cleared away at the Bethnal Green railroad bridge, a special V-2 is launched from Peenemünde out over the Baltic. Test vehicle for radio-controlled equipment for a new antiaircraft rocket, this one thunders up into the clouds, promptly refuses to respond, and heads north and a bit east. Five minutes later, Serial No. #4089 explodes on earth contact near Kalmar, Sweden.

Twisted, burned pieces of it are in a crater thirteen feet deep. As with the Bornholmers, the locals believe it is part of a German aircraft, and before the Swedish Home Guard can arrive, both adults and children cart off chunks of #4089 for souvenirs.

While the Germans make an effort to collect the rocket remains, neutral Sweden officially protests to Berlin that her airspace has been violated, that her citizens have been endangered. Quietly, Swedish authorities ask the citizens around Kalmar to bring back pieces of any wreckage.

The British don't hear of the Kalmar incident for a week or so, but Dr. Jones, for one, is overjoyed when informed. There is that "Bug River rocket" in Poland now being studied and disassembled by Anton Kocjan; now, the Kalmar V-2—or what's left of it—may become available. The Germans make a lot of noise but can do little to pry it out of a locked and guarded military shed in Stockholm.

In late June, Jones sends a pair of experts to Stockholm to examine the two tons of rocket parts. They quickly decide the material is genuine and recommend that the government work out a deal. England trades Sweden some mobile radar units for the pile of metal and wiring, and a cargo plane is dispatched. Everyone goes away happy except the Germans.

On July 16, with V-1s dropping daily in numbers ranging from three or four to forty-seven (on June 22), causing public uproar as well as considerable damage and casualties, Hitler is all smiles at a Wolf's Lair meeting of the War Council. "We are tying down hundreds of aircraft by our offensive, and bring vital relief to the Fatherland and to the battlefields in the west."

He is correct on tying down aircraft. The best way to combat the V-1 is to knock it down, one way or another. Hundreds of fighter planes are engaged in attempting to shoot down Divers or, when possible, to tuck their wing tips under the bombs' wings and flip them over, causing them to crash. Antiaircraft guns, ack-ack rockets, and barrage balloons are also engaged in the fight against the buzz bombs.

One indication of V-1 possibilities is a note that Dr. Jones leaves on his desk the afternoon of July 17.

In case I am killed during the night of 17/18 July, whoever finds this paper must take it at once to Dr. F. C. Frank, Government Communications Bureau, 54 Broadway, S.W. 1, and tell him that he will find a square concrete platform in the middle of the clearing at Blizna on Photo 3240 of PR 385 . . .

Fortunately, Dr. Jones is not killed and is present at a Crossbow Committee meeting the next day where it is decided that a V-2 attack on London is not only possible but probable. In such event, Churchill declares, he's

ready to threaten the enemy with ''large-scale gas attacks.'' Even at the height of the Battle of Britain, poison
gas bombardment was never discussed.

The situation festers in Churchill's mind for another
two days; then he lashes out at all involved for not providing more information about the V-1 and V-2 at an
earlier date. None present can remember the prime minister being more sarcastic or wrathful. No one is spared.

21. "Motyl" Field

As Churchill delivers his tongue-lashing in London, an RAF Dakota (American C-47) soars off from Brindisi, Italy, on a very special mission to a grass field near Tarnow, Poland. Flying the Allied workhorse is New Zealander Flight Lieutenant Guy Culliford; copilot and navigator is Flight Lieutenant Szrajer of the Free Polish Air Force.

Their mission this day: land at an airfield code-named Motyl, sometimes used by the Luftwaffe, and pick up the Bug River rocket parts and their escort. The latter's name is Jerzy Chmielewski, but for now he is known only as Rafael. He has bicycled about two hundred miles, avoiding Nazi patrols, with a shoulder sack of crucial parts plus the drawings.

If the Dakota is on schedule, it will land at twilight with just enough visibility left to see the field, an auxiliary spot for light aircraft. Though not visible, about four hundred resistance members, some of them armed, are in the woods surrounding Motyl throughout most of this drizzly day. They're present to ensure success of the daring mission.

In late afternoon, two German open-cockpit reconnaissance planes circle the meadow and set down on Motyl while resistance members watch nervously from the woods and debate about going out to kill the intruders. An hour goes by. The enemy pilots laugh and talk and smoke, passing time before returning to their base. Finally, not long before dark, they climb back into their aircraft and take off, unaware how close they've come to death.

Soon, the twin engines of the Dakota are heard and the waiting Poles flash lights. Culliford brings the plane down to the muddy field; Rafael quickly climbs aboard with his precious cargo, and the engines are gunned for takeoff.

Not much happens. The Dakota strains forward no more than six or eight inches. Her fixed wheels are down in the mud. The partisans push the undercarriage and tail surface to no avail as the engines roar in the twilight quiet. Any German soldiers nearby would have to hear the Pratt & Whitneys bellowing. Finally, after about twenty minutes, the partisan leader suggests they burn the plane and set up another attempt later in the week.

Another plan suits Lieutenant Culliford much better: dig out the wheels, get planks from local farms, and try again. After several tense hours, with barn doors and other planking making a runway several hundred feet long, the Dakota engines roar again, the brilliant wing lights flash on, and the aircraft finally lifts off Motyl, heading for London.

Just as the plane clears the treetops, the partisans engage an investigating Nazi patrol in a brief firefight; then they slip off into the darkness.

No screenwriter could have written a better climax to the day around Motyl, and Mr. Churchill could have found little fault with all performances. In fact, he gives it special mention in his memoirs.

Even the anticlimax, with Rafael safely in London, is tailor-made for the movies. Refusing to talk to anyone except a certain Polish general or a certain colonel, refusing to give up the bag of rocket parts, Rafael stages a one-man standoff with British intelligence. He sits on the sack of parts holding a commando knife. Anyone approaching him does so at risk of limb. Finally, the general is located and brought to Rafael. The rocket parts are peacefully transferred. So the story ends happily—except for Anton Kocjan, the young aerodynamicist back in Warsaw. Someone betrays him and he's executed by the Gestapo.

Project Big Ben, reconstruction and evaluation of both the Kalmar and Bug River rockets, begins immediately.

The prospects for England appear even more frightening when Dr. Jones submits his opinion to Crossbow that there is absolutely no defense against a supersonic missile other than hitting it on the ground before launch. Unlike the V-1, Big Ben will fall on England, unseen and unheard until the bang of breaking the sound barrier. By that time, it will be too late to run to a shelter.

Herbert Morrison, minister of home security, suggests to Churchill and the War Cabinet that plans be made to evacuate a million people from the heart of London. Without one V-2 being fired, the Germans already possess a psychological weapon of greater impact than any rocket explosion.

Peenemünde has been spared punishment by the RAF for a year mainly because intelligence analysts believe that Hydra had effectively put the rocket scientists out of business, that most of the work had been shifted to Blizna. Now they realize that the research center, despite its destroyed appearance, is still heavily involved in developing and testing weapons. The rocket that fell in Sweden did not come from Poland.

This time, the Americans are assigned the task of cratering the center. On July 18, when nine V-1s come putputting toward England, sirens wail again at Peenemünde and the string of villages along the Usedom coast. Thirty USAAF Flying Fortresses, each carrying thousand-pound bombs, roar over in daylight. Although part of Werke Süd is destroyed, the critical areas around Test Stand #7 aren't touched, and V-2s are tested two weeks later.

The bombers return twice more, using new "carpet"

techniques. Carpet bombing is laying a "carpet" of bombs. Even the soft sand heaves. The last raid occurs August 25, and as von Braun and his department heads survey the damage it is plain that Peenemünde is almost gone. The huge hangar at Test Stand #7 is a blackened shell. Next day, however, slave workers begin to rebuild, patch, and jury-rig so that the program can continue, though severely curtailed.

Morale has been slipping steadily since Hydra, reflecting the course of the war in general. The three attacks by the Fortresses these summer months drive it lower, of course, even though loss of life is small. Worse than the raids is the feeling of being choked off. Supplies are difficult to obtain, transportation irregular. The latter department needs more and more alcohol from the rocket storage tanks just to keep the trucks running. Gasoline is scarce. Food rations are tightened. There is a feeling of doom around the rocket base.

There have been radical changes since August 1. General Dr. Kammler is now head of all V-2 activity, a special commissioner with full powers to administer the entire program. The document signed by Hitler says, in part, that Kammler "acts on my orders and his directions are to be obeyed." General Dornberger has been reassigned to Berlin to develop antiaircraft weapons.

The research center is now privately run but government owned, renamed Electromechanical Industries, Karlshagen, Pomerania. The new director is from the industrial giant Siemens, though Dr. von Braun remains on the staff, since the new man knows nothing about making rockets.

Adding to the problems of further testing the still-erratic V-2 is the loss of Blizna to Russian troops. The Soviets are dismantling what little equipment was left at the Polish range, and it is already on its way to Moscow. The new testing and training facility is on the mainland south of Wolgast.

As the Russians close in from the east and the Allies

push from the west, British intelligence at last has a partial list of some of the men involved in rocket research. A captured SS trooper, formerly employed as an electrician in the supersonic wind tunnel, has named Dornberger, von Braun, Steinhoff, Hermann, the Riedels, and others prominent at Peenemünde.

22. "That's the First One!"

As the fourth summer of war wears to an end, "V-Bomb Alley," the path that the robots usually travel across Kent, Sussex, and Surrey counties to battered London, is littered with death and destruction. Between the 17th of June and September 1, a total of 5,479 people, mostly civilians, have been killed; 15,934 injured, mostly women and children. Property damage is in the millions of pounds, with an estimated 50,000 dwellings destroyed or damaged. In Croydon, three out of every four houses are losses.

Yet the flying bomb attack appears to be over this early September 1944, having reached its climax in July and August. Allied troops have now overrun most of the launching sites. In fact, the British chiefs of staff, on the 6th, say solemnly, "There should be no further damage. Allied bombers can now concentrate on other targets. . . ."

Two days later, Londoners read in the morning *Times*: "Giving a full account to a Press conference of the enemy's flying bomb attacks on this country, Mr. Duncan Sandys, M.P. [Member of Parliament], Chairman of the Flying Bomb Counter-Measures Committee, said that 92 percent of all the fatal casualties from the bomb occurred in the London area. He also revealed that during the 80-day attack, 2,300 of the 8,000 bombs launched reached the London area.

"Mr. Sandys said, 'Except possibly for a few last shots, the Battle of London is over. . . .'"

At twenty minutes to seven that evening, there is a huge explosion on Stavely Road, Chiswick-on-Thames, West London. The explosion seems to have a "double-bang." It does, in fact, as the V-2 breaks the sound barrier.

In his office, a startled Dr. Jones looks at an associate to say, "That's the first one!" He's been expecting the "double-bang" for months.

Three people are dead on Stavely Road, another seventeen injured. V-2s have finally arrived, the result of thirteen years of research and an outlay of more than 500 million Deutschmarks. Sixteen seconds later, another V-2 crashes down on Parndon Woods, near Epping.

The rockets, fueled by eight tons of alcohol and liquid oxygen, had sped from the launch site at Haagsche Bosch, a wooded park on the outskirts of The Hague, Netherlands, crossing the lower North Sea in less than six minutes. Each carried two thousand pounds of explosives. The first V-2s had been fired earlier toward liberated Paris.

The mobile launching units in Holland consist of three *Meillerwagens*, each loaded with one V-2. An armored half-track pulls the *wagen* and also transports the firing crew. Three tank trucks supply the liquid oxygen, alcohol, and auxiliary fuels; on another truck is an electric generator. After selection of the launching site, under normal circumstances no more than four hours is required to fuel, arm, and fire the missile. Hitler's plan of permanent bunkers such as at Watten and Wizernes has long been abandoned.

Secrecy is immediately clamped on the two explosions in the greater London area, and there are rumors in Chiswick that the Stavely Road explosion was a gas main. No V-1 was heard. Official spokesmen say vaguely, "Yes, a gas main might have blown."

On the heels of the V-2 attack, the worry is that this

latest *wunder* weapon might cause civilian panic. Evacuation is still a possibility.

Unlike the V-1, with its motorbike noise as a warning, slow speed, and final dive to earth, the V-2 is split-second death. However, it is soon difficult to determine which weapon is the more frightening. If a person is in position to hear the final "whoosh" of the V-2 before impact, there's no worry of survival. Death is usually instant.

Twenty-four of the missiles fall on England, mostly in the London area, during September. The only defense against them, as Dr. Jones has predicted, is to bomb the launch sites, and raids are immediately directed against every known or suspected V-2 firing place. Low-level fighter-bomber attacks work best. However, the mobile *Meillerwagens*, moving quickly to a road crossing, launching, then moving to another, prove to be elusive targets. Only a lucky hit ever destroys a missile on the ground.

Von Braun and the personnel still working at Peenemünde learn of the opening London attack but have little to say about it. Internal Gestapo spies seem to be everywhere, and any comment might be dangerous. Von Braun in particular is very careful now about what he says. His weeks in prison at Stettin are still fresh in his memory.

Despite the destruction from the American raids, a V-2 launch is scheduled for early October, although there is concern about the availability of liquid oxygen. The Peenemünde plant was destroyed in the raid of August 25, and only seven such plants now exist in Germany.

There are still problems with the missile, and a number have blown up on launch sites. Yet sixty-three are successfully sent toward England in the first two weeks of October. In response, hedgehopping Spitfire attacks seeking out the *Meillerwagens* and tank trucks make more sense than big bomber raids, and five hundred such missions are flown before bad weather shuts them down.

Hitler orders Antwerp, main entry harbor of Allied army supplies, to be attacked equally with London, and V-1s as well as V-2s begin crashing into the huge seaport up the Scheldt River.

A few days before Christmas, von Braun drives to his parents' Silesia farm estate, Weisenthal, near the Czechoslovakian border, to persuade them to leave before the Russians appear at the front gate demanding horses and cattle. He tells them he plans to find a way to surrender to the Americans; that he'll take his younger brother Magnus with him wherever he goes.

But the elder von Braun decides to stay on the farm and take his chances. As a local leader, the baron believes that he can be of help to neighboring farmers when the inevitable occurs. Father, mother, and son embrace, knowing they may never see one another again.

Though little work can be accomplished, von Braun returns to Peenemünde to await instructions from Kammler. The SS command refuses even to discuss evacuation of the almost totally demolished center. Two engineers who advocated leaving have been arrested and executed. They now hang from burnt trees along the main road inside the fence, signs pinned on their chests: *"I was too cowardly to defend the homeland."*

23. To the Mountains

Most of January is bitterly cold and cloudy, adding to the plight of frightened, half-frozen refugees as thousands flee from Russian armies invading the eastern provinces. One hundred and eighty Soviet divisions are attacking East Prussia and Poland.

Mostly old men, women, and children, traveling with wheelbarrows, pushcarts, horsecarts, anything with wheels, the refugees take the ferry at Swinemünde, shuffle silently up the road, turn south at the center's fence, and then go on to cross the Peene at Wolgast. The rocket makers watch them in despair, unable to help.

Mid-month, von Braun holds a secret meeting with Steinhoff, Walter Riedel, and others to discuss surrendering to the Allies. Never to Russia. Looking to the future, the scientists realize neither England nor France can afford a long-range space program. That leaves the U.S.A. Each man will make his own decision when the time comes.

The expected signal from Nordhausen to leave Peenemünde arrives January 31 by teletype, and von Braun immediately summons all department heads and key staff members to tell them that General Kammler has just ordered all the important defense projects to be shifted to central Germany. The department heads are given two hours in which to submit a preliminary estimate of how many personnel will go, including families, and how much equipment.

Though the pound of Soviet artillery cannot be heard as yet, ancient German fears of the Russian bear dominate much of the thinking.

Nordhausen is 250 miles to the south, over clogged roads and railway lines now continually bombed and strafed by Allied aircraft. Made only at night, the trip to the Harz Mountains will be no more or less dangerous, or chaotic, than any other movement in Germany in this period.

Even before the planning estimates can reach his office, von Braun is informed by the area military commander, a Wehrmacht general, that all male personnel must remain at Peenemünde and join the *Volkssturm*, the People's Army, to defend the island to the "last man."

Von Braun considers this a "stupid order" and quickly decides to obey the hated Kammler instead. Area commands and chains of command are disintegrating daily; authority is splitting and overlapping. Conflicting orders are an everyday occurrence. A number of high-ranking officers are now concerned only with saving their own skins. Others, fanatics, are ready to die. This time, von Braun believes it is wiser to go along with the SS and use the power of Kammler to advantage. The alternative is capture or death at the hands of the Red Army.

Preliminary estimates indicate that some five thousand personnel should go to Nordhausen, along with thousands of tons of assorted vital equipment. Transfer work begins.

A transportation expert frantically rounds up information on available railroad cars, trucks, gasoline, tires, and barges for twelve thousand tons of freight. Others make decisions on exactly what scientific equipment to take, what to destroy, what papers are necessary, which can be burned. Leave the Russians nothing of value!

While all this is going on during the first few days of February, a twenty-eight-year-old U.S. Army ordnance major named Robert Staver arrives in London on a very secret and special mission. He has a long list of German scientists known to be working, or to have worked, on the V-2. Compiled by both U.S. and British intelligence experts, Staver's so-called Black List is headed with the name of Wernher von Braun. His Gray List is composed of engineers, less important but still of value.

Staver's sole job is to facilitate the seizure of rocket scientists, along with equipment, before or after the armistice is signed. The U.S. Joint Chiefs of Staff believe that the scientists pose a "dangerous threat in the future" and do not want them to fall into the eager arms of the Soviets, in particular. The ALSOS Mission, organized the previous year, has begun.

Russia, of course, also has a special committee on the trail of rocket secrets. Even further behind than the U.S. in space research, the Soviets got little of importance from capturing Blizna. They had agreed to share any Blizna secrets and equipment with the Americans and British, but what is turned over amounts to some boxes of useless aircraft parts. U.S. officials will soon do likewise to the Russians.

There'll also be competition from England in the race for the rockets, and even among the American service branches. Both the U.S. Navy and the Army Air Force will covet von Braun, his associates, and their rockets. Staver and his superiors want the missile booty and personnel for the U.S. Army and none other.

February 4, spurred by a false rumor that the Communists are less than a hundred miles away, von Braun flies to Nordhausen to make a survey of possible locations for various research units. No matter how hopeless the cause, he must go through the motions of helping to make war.

Next day, loading of the railroad cars begins. Packing is the only worthwhile chore on the whole battered island. Travel light, the families are told. Just clothing and a few possessions.

The uncomfortable, even scary, alliance with the SS suddenly becomes a plus for the move. Specially prepared papers, letterheads, and passes specifically point up the rocket makers' close association with SS Reichs-führer Himmler. A meaningless designation of *VZBV* is stenciled a foot high on the sides of vehicles, railroad cars, and boxes of freight.

When asked what *VZBV* means, the ready answer is, *A new secret weapons agency of the SS, not to be counter-manded except by Himmler himself.* In all the confusion, it just may work.

The first train—twelve cars carrying over five hundred personnel and their families, plus four boxcars—chuffs away on the frigid night of February 17, bound for Nord-hausen. Blackout curtains pulled down tight, bodies jammed into the compartments, the train gets through to the mountains without being attacked.

Fortunately, von Braun returns from the south just in time to accompany the first convoy of trucks, loaded with freight and some of the families. His presence is needed almost immediately. The convoy runs into an army roadblock at the town of Eberswalde, within the command area of the fanatic general whose orders to remain on Use-dom are being disobeyed.

The officer at the barrier tells von Braun that no civil-ian traffic is permitted on the road. The danger is that he might check with his superiors; the convoy, emblazoned with *VZBV*, will likely be turned back.

The normally quiet-voiced, even-tempered von Braun begins to shout at the major, informing him that *VZBV* stands for *Vorhaben zur Besonderen Verwendung* (Proj-ect for Special Dispositions), a top secret relocation or-dered by SS Reichsführer Himmler. Now, does the major really want to check with the SS Reichsführer?

The major obviously does not want to make that check and angrily waves the convoy onward. Even admirals and generals are very careful about checking with Him-mler in late winter, 1945.

By mid-March, the population of Peenemünde num-bers less than a thousand and will decrease even more.

All the important equipment has been removed and is either en route to Nordhausen by truck or rail or sitting on docks in the port of Lubeck awaiting barges. Meanwhile, the former residents of Usedom are in the Harz Mountains, settling into villages around Nordhausen, preparing to go back to work when possible.

Headquarters for von Braun is an abandoned power plant in the cotton-mill town of Bleicherode, west of Nordhausen. He plans to go ahead with research and development that will have little to do with weaponry; his various units begin setting up in empty garages, warehouses, even a castle. Many personnel say it is all futile; they'll be in enemy hands within a few weeks. Von Braun points out that they can be in Gestapo hands in a few hours unless they remain active and close-lipped.

General Dornberger has moved his weapons development staffs to Bad Sachsa, also near Nordhausen, and stays in close touch with von Braun, though the general no longer has any responsibility for the V-2 program.

On the night of March 16, von Braun heads for Berlin to argue for rocket funds, futile or not, and is asleep at 3:00 A.M. on the Autobahn when his young driver dozes off. The car swerves over an embankment, rolls, and crashes. Both survive the accident, but the scientist's shoulder is shattered and his arm broken. But he's lucky to be alive and is carted off to the hospital.

At the end of the week, Hitler issues his infamous "scorched-earth" directive ordering the SS and Wehrmacht to destroy everything and anything of value as the enemy approaches. Germany is to be charred.

A few days later, von Braun demands to be let out of the hospital to celebrate his thirty-third birthday, and during the party he and Dornberger agree that the tons of documents and blueprints that led to the first A-4 must somehow survive the scorching. Over sixty-five thousand drawings were involved in the first successful A-4.

Von Braun promises the general, "I'll find a way to hide them."

Major Staver, in London, as well as a number of scientists and military officers in the U.S.A., would have been very happy to hear that conversation.

24. The Vengeance Express

The last successful V-2 to land on British soil drives down on Orphington, in Kent, at 4:45 P.M., March 27, ending six months of rocket attack. More than 2,500 people have been killed, more than six thousand injured, by the terror weapon. A few more are fired at Antwerp in a last gasp of Kammler's V-2 troops, who now become infantrymen.

None of the Peenemünde rocket makers is aware of the final launches.

Easter Sunday morning a rumor sweeps through Bleicherode that American tanks have been sighted twelve miles away, causing a half dozen staff members to rush to von Braun's house for instructions. Though the rumor proves to be false—the tanks are almost a hundred miles away—von Braun decides it is time to hide the V-2 documents and gives that chore to personal aide Dieter Huzel and to Bernhard Tessman, designer of many Peenemünde facilities.

Huzel will later recall von Braun saying, "Probably the best possibility is an old mine or cave—something of that sort. Other than that, I have no specific thoughts. There is just no time to lose."

Not long after Huzel and Tessman depart to begin rounding up the technical papers, von Braun is summoned by General Kammler to Nordhausen. Arm extended in the air like a wing, torso cast almost to his waist, pain slicing at him every moment, von Braun endures the short ride and is then informed more pain is coming. He'll be leaving the area, along with his five hundred top scientists and engineers, to go to the National or Alpine Redoubt, a specially secured stronghold in the Bavarian Alps, for reasons of safety.

The broad-shouldered, lean, movie-star-type general, looking and acting as if he might be on the verge of a mental breakdown, says the Peenemünde group will be guarded by special SD troops (intelligence and espionage arm of the SS) and that a former army camp at Oberammergau will be used for headquarters and further research.

Kammler's own twelve-car train, the sleek *Vergeltungs-Express* (Vengeance Express), will transport the rocket personnel and guards. No families will be permitted to go.

Von Braun listens to Kammler, uneasiness growing every minute. He's quite willing to go to the Alps for "safety" but is also worried that the general may have thoughts of holding the scientists hostage, exchanging them to the Allies for his own life. Von Braun knows that as many as thirty thousand prisoners of one type or another have been employed on V-2 projects. Some are here in Nordhausen; others are out at Camp Dora at Mittelwerke. Many have already died. Kammler is certain to be arrested and is a likely candidate for the gallows.

Von Braun had heard, vaguely, of a plan for the top officials of the Nazi government to retreat to a heavily fortified, well-supplied redoubt in the Alps, there to regroup and begin guerrilla warfare with crack troops, finally unleashing new weapons to conquer all enemies. An insane plan, von Braun had thought at the time he heard of it. True or not, von Braun believes that Kammler is much too clever to think it will ever happen.

Nonetheless, he has little choice except to obey Kammler. Aside from attempting to defect to the approaching enemy, the other scientists have no choice either. Strength may lie in sticking together. As he is driven back to Bleicherode this Sunday, when the churches are trying to celebrate Easter, he thinks how ironic it is that Kammler has picked quaint Oberammergau, home of the world-famous Passion play, the story of the suffering, death, and resurrection of Christ, to house the makers of the V-2. During peacetime, the play is performed every ten years by the villagers.

Arriving home, von Braun phones General Dornberger to tell him of Kammler's latest move, and Dornberger quickly makes his own plans to shift to the Alps, taking along a hundred troops that he knows are personally loyal to him. He, too, suspects that Kammler may be thinking "hostage."

Though treacherous, Hans Kammler is also a remarkable man, in Dornberger's opinion. Prior to the war he had never served a day of military service, yet he now has the rank of major general. Several years previously, no one had ever heard of Dr. Hans Kammler; now he is at Hitler's personal beck and call, trusted by the Führer.

Dornberger has discovered other things about Kammler since the past September. Twice Dornberger has met him on the Autobahn past midnight to discuss weapons. Kammler would awaken sleeping aides with a tommy-gun burst. "No need for them to sleep. I can't!"

Dornberger has also learned why Kammler's chief of staff always walks ten paces behind the general with a loaded machine pistol. The chief of staff has orders to kill Kammler with a burst to the back of the head rather than let him be captured.

On April 2, von Braun and the five hundred scientists and engineers selected for the Oberammergau redoubt pack for an indefinite stay in the Alps. On the same day, Dieter Huzel and Bernhard Tessman are sorting, selecting, and crating fourteen tons of V-2 paperwork gathered from the Nordhausen-Bleicherode area. Much of it had already been gathered for the move from Peenemünde.

Into labeled wooden boxes goes work dating back to

Kummersdorf-West. Papers that aren't considered of value are burnt. The two men get only three hours' sleep from noon Easter Sunday to late evening of the next day, when Kammler's Vengeance Express begins boarding passengers for the snow peaks.

Standing along the Nordhausen station platform are thirty or so SD guards; another sixty are already on the train. Goodbyes are tearful, as many of the scientists do not believe they'll ever see their families again.

Still in great pain, unable to manuever around with the arm and body cast, von Braun is spared the train ride south. He leaves Bleicherode in the back seat of a car driven by an SD soldier.

25. Mission Accomplished

Rain is falling on central Germany the chill morning of April 3 as a small car leads a convoy of three big Opel trucks toward the village of Clausthal, headquarters for the area's many mines. Huzel, passenger in the soldier-driven car, wants to ask officials if they know of a large cave or mine that might be used to store army "personnel" records.

Tessman is in the cab of the first truck, also driven by a soldier. Five other enlisted men are along to drive and help unload the cargo. Two of the trucks have large trailers attached.

American fighter planes are roaming around freely, looking for targets despite the rain, and the convoy has to pull up under trees several times to keep from being strafed.

In a valley about five miles from Clausthal, north and west toward Hannover, Huzel finally decides that the safest, smartest thing to do is to go on ahead, question the officials, find a hiding place, then return. Wandering around the countryside with three big trucks is asking for trouble.

With the Americans reported only thirty miles away, what is urgently needed is an inactive mine tunneled into a mountainside. Vertical shafts and elevators can't be used because mine personnel would be needed to help store the materials. Also, Huzel plans to dynamite the entrance, sealing it.

He is told that no inactive mines or horizontal shafts are located in the Clausthal area and to go to Goslar, fifteen miles away. At Goslar, officials claim that all suitable mines are already filled with government records from Berlin. But, one official remembers, ''There is an old horizontal shaft at Dornten. . . .'' The official even offers to go along to the village, ten miles away on a lonely secondary road. The little car is off again.

Huzel is becoming more frustrated by the hour with what seems to be an impossible task. By now it is late afternoon, and as they drive past Dornten the first thing Huzel sees is the tower of a vertical shaft. Beyond, however, is an abandoned horizontal shaft sunk into a low hillside.

Soon, the mine's elderly caretaker escorts them into the darkness, leading the way with lamp glow. About three hundred yards along the shaft, the old man points to another tunnel, saying that a large room with a steel door, formerly used for explosives, lies in that direction. Another hundred yards later, when the door creaks open, Huzel sees a dry, perfect place for the rocket records.

After returning first to Goslar to drop off the helpful official, Huzel heads back for the valley where his small convoy is hidden. In a few minutes, the trucks are rolling again, this time bound for a quarry five miles from Dornten, where the Opels sit throughout the next day, hidden from Allied planes.

At nightfall, Huzel and Tessman lock the eight soldiers into the back of the first truck for the ride to the Dornten mine. If the soldiers are captured by the enemy, they won't be able to reveal the exact location of the shaft. Just outside it, all hands begin to load the many boxes onto flatcars pulled by a small electric locomotive for the three-hundred-yard ride to the offshoot tunnel. From there on, it is back-and-shoulder work to haul the boxes the final hundred yards to the explosives room.

The procedure is repeated three times, ending about eleven o'clock the next morning, everyone totally exhausted. But the priceless rocket data have been preserved.

In the afternoon, while Huzel, Tessman, and the soldiers are sleeping in Dornten, the caretaker dynamites the entrance to the tunnel. Next day, Huzel and Tessman revisit the shaft and aren't satisfied with the amount of rock that fell. They ask for total blockage of the tunnel and the caretaker fires off more charges.

Knowing that the papers are now relatively safe, they depart for Bleicherode only hours before advance elements of the U.S. Ninth Army thump and throb through little Dornten.

Next day, General Dornberger heads for the Alps with his staff, on orders from Kammler. Even more than von Braun, Dornberger is concerned about what Kammler may do at Oberammergau. SD soldiers are now accompanying Dornberger, though he has that small contingent of his own loyalists along.

On April 11, four days after Huzel and Tessman complete their mission, task forces of the U.S. Third Armored Division roll into partially destroyed Nordhausen. Though alerted by intelligence to expect something unusual in the Harz Mountains area, the commanders aren't at all prepared for what is at Niedersachswerfen and under Kohnstein Mountain. General Truman Boudinot has never heard of the rocket assembly plant or Mittelwerke's Camp Dora, and had no prior information that another concentration camp existed at Nordhausen.

Mittelwerke and both concentration camps have been abandoned in panic by SS guards the day before, and General Boudinot, a hardened, tough veteran of fighting that had begun on Normandy beaches, cannot believe the scene of horror in front of him. At the Nordhausen camp, as many as five thousand corpses are scattered grotesquely around. Some in piles, some naked, some in tat-

tered striped pajamas. Fleeing, the guards had disobeyed
Kammler's orders to cremate the evidence.

About a thousand half-starved, babbling rocket assem-
blers still survive, and those able to, stagger toward the
tankmen.

On to Mittelwerke, at Niedersachswerfen, go the
American officers, and more babbling Jewish survivors,
with arms and legs "like pipestems," dressed in the
filthy pajamas, lead them into the main tunnel. The
Americans are dumfounded to see the neat V-2 assembly
lines stretching deep into the mountain. Nothing has been
touched; all the machinery seems to be in working order.
There are hundreds of missiles.

Soon a message clicks out to an ordnance intelligence
colonel in Paris that the Timberlake Division has captured a whole factory of V-2s. The colonel, Holger Toftoy, one of the bosses of that young Major Staver who
had arrived in London with the Black List, has a request
for one hundred of the rockets. They are to be sent, as
soon as possible, to the U.S. Army Proving Ground at
White Sands, New Mexico.

How to get the V-2s out from under the noses of both
the British and the approaching Russians is Colonel Toftoy's problem.

In an unfortunate agreement so far as the army is concerned, President Roosevelt and Prime Minister Churchill had agreed to let Russia have a large portion of
Germany no matter whose armies arrived first. Mittelwerke is in that Soviet Zone, and according to the Yalta
decision the Red Army already owns those missiles and
all the machinery, even has jurisdiction over the scientists and technicians said to be in the Nordhausen area.
Toftoy and his superiors do not intend to carry out that
agreement, no matter what Roosevelt and Churchill have
signed. Neither of those leaders knew what would be
found in the Harz Mountains.

And at this point, neither Toftoy nor Staver are aware
that the Black List scientists are no longer in north or cen-

tral Germany. The forty-five hundred lower-level technicians left behind, both military and civilian, have scattered into the many villages throughout the mountains. They're in hiding, of course.

26. PFC Schneiker

General Kammler's SD contingent that escorted the Peenemünde group to the Alps is now guarding the former Alpine regimental camp at Oberammergau, which is ringed with barbed wire. Movement of the scientists is restricted, and although they are told that everything is for their "safety," there is an inescapable feeling of prison.

Having arrived safely in the auto, still in much pain, still firmly believing that he and his colleagues are little more than hostages, von Braun nonetheless hopes to continue limited research work. Although Allied planes are frequently overhead, it is unlikely they'll bomb the mountain villages unless German troops begin to occupy them.

Reports of the land war remain confusing and unreliable, and von Braun has no idea which Allied troops are approaching the villages, if any. For mind and body, once again the best solution for all is to stay busy and hope American tanks will be first to arrive.

Oberammergau perches in snowy mountains under the towering crag of the Kofel, with its huge wooden cross on top. Far away is the Zugspitze, ten thousand feet up. Goatherds, bells ringing, still go through the red-roofed village in early morning, war or no war. It is a storybook hamlet of wood-carvers and players in the saga of Christ. Their last performance was in 1938. Only death and destruction could cause this village to play host to men who created death and destruction.

One huge anxiety of von Braun's is relieved April 11 when Bernhard Tessman arrives in camp to say that the V-2 papers have been properly buried. Besides Tessman and Huzel, the only other person who knows the location is Karl Fischer, an administrator both at Peenemünde and Nordhausen. Tessman and Huzel felt they should tell someone in case they were both killed en route to Bavaria. Huzel is still on the road to Oberammergau, having detoured to the rubble of Berlin.

Though General Kammler is in Oberammergau, he makes no contact with von Braun until the following week. Summoned to an inn run by a cast member of the Passion play, the scientist finds a relaxed SS general, not the wild-eyed, nearly irrational man he last saw in Nordhausen. Kammler offers von Braun a drink and then inquires about his general health and the healing of the accident injuries, about the welfare of the scientists in the camp, about the prospects of getting back into a full schedule. The general seems genuinely concerned, certainly not threatening. He turns on the charm of which he is so capable. It makes him all the more frightening.

Finally, advising von Braun that other duties are sending him away for a while, the general names a Major Kummer to take his place in command of the Alpine group. Kammler also reaffirms his faith in Germany's ultimate triumph, and after "Heiling Hitler," dismisses the scientist.

Next day, von Braun and Ernst Steinhoff pay a visit to Major Kummer, seeing an opportunity to slip out of the immediate SD grasp. After buttering up the major, who isn't too happy over his new assignment, they express grave concern over the Allied aircraft that are crisscrossing the Alps. If one were to make a lucky hit on the camp, Germany's top weapons makers could be wiped out.

The major ponders that briefly and then asks how the

danger might be avoided. Don't keep all the personnel in one place, von Braun cleverly suggests. Split them up between surrounding villages. The major finally agrees.

Within a few days, the scientists begin to spread out to twenty-two villages at distances of five to twenty-odd miles from Oberammergau. Although some SD guards go along, several to each group, the grasp is loosened. It will be more difficult to hold them all hostage, should that be the plan. Dr. von Braun and his brother Magnus take up residence in Weilheim, about twenty miles from the camp, without guards.

But the accident injuries and the mental stress of months finally send von Braun to the hospital in nearby Sonthofen. The pain is constant and he can no longer function. Without anesthetics, the arm is rebroken and von Braun is bedded down in traction until a second operation can be performed. He is, in fact, wired up and helpless the next day when Thunderbolts of the U.S. Tactical Air Force do the unexpected—strafe and bomb several of the mountain towns. Sonthofen receives a twenty-minute treatment, bombs falling close enough to blow out the window in von Braun's room.

After the raid, rumors are thicker than ever that the enemy is approaching, and there is no reason to doubt them. The aerial attack intensifies the feeling of doom among the scientists cloistered in the Alps, who see their options as imprisonment by the Americans or the Russians or perhaps death by Kammler's troops.

Most of the scientists, including von Braun, have considered their roles in making the rockets and realize that there is a slim possibility they may be charged with war crimes, though there is no legal basis for such action. They are well aware of the inhumane treatment of the slave laborers, of the starvation and death in the missile-connected camps. They do not know how the enemy will react to that discovery.

After more than a week in traction, von Braun has had ample chance to consider all of the future possibilities, and the one he still fears most is from the absent General Dr. Hans Kammler.

During this same week of April, most of the remaining personnel are evacuated from Peenemünde, most going by ship to Kiel, though the Russians have not shown up along their probable advance through north Poland. Von Braun, however, has no knowledge of what is occurring on Usedom. All communication has been cut off.

On the 25th, he's awakened from a deep sleep to find a uniformed man by his bedside and is greatly relieved to see a Red Cross insignia rather than an SD armband. The medic has orders from General Dornberger to move Dr. von Braun to Oberjoch, a village to the west, higher in the Alps, not a likely target for Thunderbolts. Dornberger also sends a message: The French are closing in on Sonthofen; leave while you can.

A new torso and arm cast is fitted, and von Braun slides into the ambulance along with Magnus for the ride to Oberjoch, one of the Alpine jewels, both a summer and winter resort.

The ambulance pulls to a halt in front of Haus Ingeborg, the best hotel in the village, and the von Braun brothers are greeted by Dornberger and a few others of the Peenemünde team. In the lobby, von Braun spots a number of SD men but, surprisingly, they are now in regular army uniforms. Kammler isn't present. Dornberger says quietly, "I'll tell you later."

Von Braun feels much safer in Oberjoch.

How many German officials and military chiefs have ever heard of the Alpine Redoubt—or believe what they have heard—is not known this April of 1945. However, this strategy, supposedly a creation of Hitler's, with fanatic troops and underground factories, *wunder* weapons and guerrillas, is very definitely believed by Allied intelligence. And by no less than General Eisenhower himself. Lodged in the snow peaks, such a force would be capable of holding out for a long time, extracting many Allied casualties.

It certainly seems plausible this spring. The Nazi movement began in Bavaria, and Hitler, Goering, and party minister Martin Bormann have residences in the mountains of Berchtesgaden, guarded by the SS and hooked together by tunnels. Hitler's Eagle's Nest is known to be on the summit of a peak at Obersalzberg. An Alpine "last stand" for all of them seems within reason.

Two weeks before von Braun's ambulance journey to Oberjoch, Eisenhower had decided to strike at the Alpine Redoubt, wherever and whatever it was, before the Germans had a chance to pull back to it. He ordered the U.S. Seventh Army to advance to southern Bavaria and link up with the U.S. Fifth, coming up from Italy; he further ordered the French First Army to drive toward the Alps. Whatever it was, Ike wanted it destroyed.

As Dornberger—now out of uniform—von Braun, his brother, and the others at Oberjoch sit in the warm sun, the general asks himself, "Have the last few years been nothing but a bad dream?"

Above them tower the snow-covered Allgäu Mountains. The view is breathtaking. "Far below us it was already spring. Even on our high mountain pass the first flowers of spring were thrusting through the melting snow. It was so infinitely peaceful here," he later writes.

No longer are the thirty Kammler troops who were ordered to "guard" Dornberger a problem. Wanting to avoid a firefight with his own troops, billeted near the hotel, Dornberger had persuaded the SDs to lay down arms and change into regular army uniforms. As members of the SD, they might be shot by the Americans, certainly by the Russians. As regular troops, they'd simply go off to POW camps. The general did not advise them on how to get rid of their SS tattoos.

Awaiting capture, the small group of rocket refugees in posh Haus Ingeborg while away the time in fine spring weather getting suntans, taking walks down the mountain paths, speculating endlessly as to what will happen to them and their work.

War is full of irony and some situations defy words, and this is one—the creators of the V-2 lolling on pads in the Alpine sun, wrapped in mountain silence, contemplating the future, already having turned away from the past.

Late evening of May 1, speculation ends in another chapter of past and future:

> Radio Berlin—our Führer, Adolf Hitler, fighting to the last breath against Bolshevism, fell for Germany this afternoon in his operational headquarters of the Reich Chancellery.

Von Braun suggests that they all surrender voluntarily to the Americans without waiting for that inevitable demand. Voluntary surrender by any career soldier, for any reason, is always painful to consider, but Dornberger, more engineer than military officer, finally agrees that the "rocket effort should be put into the right hands." Of course, Dornberger and the scientists now have little to say about the final disposition of anything.

The only person at Haus Ingeborg who speaks passably good English is Magnus, and it is agreed he should try to make contact with any U.S. forces in the area while the others remain in the hotel. Instructed what to say by Dornberger and his elder brother, Magnus sets off early the next morning on a bicycle.

At that moment, the French First Army is three hours to the west, the American Fifth is farther away, and the Seventh Army's Forty-fourth Infantry Division, moving swiftly south from Munich, has already bypassed Oberjoch. But there is a small unit in the area, an antitank company moving warily along the road nestled in the pine slopes. All of the units in the Alps have been expecting vicious attacks out of the redoubt that existed only in the imagination of Hitler and a few top officials.

Magnus is only a hundred yards from the hotel, peddling downhill, when he makes contact with Private First Class Fred Schneiker of Sheboygan, Wisconsin. Magnus quickly explains that the men responsible for the V-2 are in a hotel just up the road and want to surrender.

Schneiker speaks German, and the conversation is in both English and German. The Pfc. has heard of the V-2 attacks on London and Antwerp but knows nothing beyond that, certainly not of the Black List and the ALSOS Mission. "I think you're nuts," Schneiker flatly tells Magnus, not believing him.

Even though Schneiker thinks Magnus is crazy, he takes the German to his officer in charge. The officer doesn't share Schneiker's opinion of Magnus's sanity, fearing instead that the story might be an invitation to ambush. So he declines to go up to the hotel, instructing Schneiker to take Magnus to the Forty-fourth Division's counter-intelligence headquarters in Reutte, not too far away.

CIC officers do know of a plan to interrogate German scientists but find it hard to believe that the V-2 makers, one a general officer, are in Oberjoch. Magnus is given safe-conduct passes for all and returns to Haus Ingeborg about two o'clock.

Dornberger had shed his uniform the week before and now strips his leather coat of all insignia. He finds an ordinary civilian fedora in the village and purchases it.

Not long after, three gray passenger sedans pull away from Oberjoch and roll for CIC headquarters in Reutte. The general in mufti, von Braun and his brother, Dieter Huzel, and Bernhard Tessman, who can show the Americans the way to the blocked tunnel in Dornten, are among the passengers.

For them the war is over.

In not long a time, the war is over for General Dr. Hans Kammler as well. He commits suicide.

27. The Russians Are Coming!
The Russians Are Coming!

During the first week of May, as von Braun and Dornberger soak up sun in the Alps, there are sounds of explosions behind the rocket center fence on Usedom. Inside it, members of the *Volkssturm*, the People's Army, are blowing up machinery.

The Reds are coming!

And on May 5, 1945, they arrive. Major Anatoli Vavilov, commanding an infantry unit of General Rokossovsky's Second White Russian Army, approaches the boundary at Karlshagen. Behind the chain links are a few die-hard SS troops and a few very scared civilians.

Some shots break the quiet and then a white flag is waved, either by the civilians or SS guards. It matters little; war has long been over by the river Peene. Vavilov enters with his soldiers to occupy the shambles and soon reports to his superiors that Peenemünde is "75 percent destroyed." The percentage is actually higher.

From the charred ghost town of the Siedlung, untouched since the Hydra raid of 1943, to the cratered Test Stand #7, the whole of the research center is a tangle of blackened, twisted steel and piles of charred wood.

The Russians, hungry for anything that might aid their own space flight research, had hoped they'd find not only intact V-2s but some of the scientists who had made them. Wreckage is what they have now, and the caretaker technicians that day are of little value. However, they are put into service dismantling any partially usable machinery for transport back to the Soviet Union.

Interrogation provides information that all the important documents were removed, and also provides the names of all the German scientists involved. Over the next several days, the Russians learn that the real treasures of Peenemünde are now in the Harz Mountains.

That area becomes the priority target for their own special committee on the track of rocket secrets as Grand Admiral Doenitz surrenders Germany to the Allies, unconditionally, at 2:41 A.M., May 7, 1945.

Afterwards

No sooner had the war ended between the Allies and Germany when it began all over again between the victors for political and military spoils, and of the latter, no spoil was given higher priority than rocket technology. Soviet agents had already stolen the atom bomb secret, and missiles were next on the list.

As a result of Yalta, there could be no denying the Russians access to Mittelwerke and other rocket facilities in the Nordhausen area. Though Churchill disagreed, advisers to President Truman, successor to the late President Roosevelt, told him that he must live up to the agreements for the sake of future good relations. American troops would have to pull back by June 21.

So men like Major Staver and Colonel Toftoy, intent on sharing as little as they could with the Russians, had their work cut out for them: ship the one hundred missiles as well as the "Dornten papers" to White Sands, and above all, spirit the most important rocket scientists, beginning with Dr. von Braun, out of Germany and away from the clutches of the Soviets.

It was mostly accomplished. Three hundred boxcars of missile components were whisked away from America's war partners, as were all of the Dornten papers. And in the initial phases of Operation Overcast (sometimes known as Paperclip), more than a hundred of the top Peenemünde scientists were sent to America. Eventually, more than four hundred of the Usedom team entered the U.S.A. to work in the space program.

Although gaining Mittelwerke intact and tons of research equipment in the Nordhausen area, plus quite a few lesser-level scientists and engineers, Russia did not fare as well. The United States clearly "stole the cream" from the Red bear. England wound up with a pair of V-2s and little else.

Dr. von Braun, of course, became America's leading space figure and did indeed live to see a man put on the moon, a lot of that voyage due to his personal efforts dating back to Rocketfield, Berlin. General Dornberger, after being imprisoned in England for two years, was released and came to the United States as an employee of Bell Aerosystems.

There are those who still say that the German scientists should have been tried and punished for their war involvement instead of being rewarded with high-paying jobs in the American space and missile programs. Reality says that the Russians would have had no such thoughts or compunctions. *Sputnik* went into space first despite the fact that the United States had the scientific cream.

The space programs of all nations really began in Auburn, Massachusetts, when Dr. Robert Goddard launched his first liquid-fuel rocket in 1926. That cabbage patch deserves to be called "The Kitty Hawk of Space," but it was on the island of Usedom—Rocket Island—that the technology was developed. War, for all its death, destruction, and tragedy, remains the chief instrument of technical progress.

Germany's V-weapons, however, are now judged to be the result of ingrained German "romance" rather than military practicality. They appealed to a need the Germans felt at that time for *wunder* weapons. Had the same amount of effort and money been put into conventional bombing, experts estimate, England would have suffered much more.

Even General Eisenhower's appraisal, "It seemed

likely that, if the German had succeeded in perfecting and using these weapons six months earlier than he did, our invasion of Europe would have proved exceedingly difficult, perhaps impossible,'' is now judged as overstatement.

As the full story of the V-weapons emerged, one thing was certain: Adolf Hitler hurt the program more than he helped it. They were never ''Hitler's weapons'' as was believed.

The island of Usedom is now part of Communist East Germany, and a Warsaw Pact installation is on the northwest tip, replacing Luftwaffe West. Some of the rocket center ruins still exist, though the woods have crept back toward the Baltic Sea.

Bibliography

Baumbach, Werner. *Life and Death of the Luftwaffe*. New York: Coward-McCann, Inc., 1960.

Bergaust, Erik. *Reaching for the Stars*. New York: Doubleday & Co., 1960.

Cooksley, Peter G. *Flying Bomb*. London: Robert Hale, 1979.

David, Heather M. *Wernher von Braun*. New York: G.P. Putnam's Sons, 1967.

Dornberger, Walter. *V-2*, with introduction by Willy Ley. New York: Viking Press, Inc., 1954.

Gartmann, H. *The Men Behind the Space Rocket*. New York: McKay, 1956.

Goddard, Robert H. *Rocket Development*. New York: Prentice-Hall, Inc., 1948.

Huzel, Dieter. *Peenemünde to Canaveral*. New York: Prentice-Hall, 1956.

Irving, David. *The Mare's Nest*. Boston: Little, Brown Co., 1965.

Johnson, Brian. *The Secret War*. London: Arrow Books, 1979.

Joubert, Sir Phillip. *Rocket*. London: Hutchinson, 1957.

Jones, R. V. *Most Secret War*. London: Hamish Hamilton, Ltd., 1978.

Ley, Willy. *Rockets, Missiles and Space Travel*. New York: The Viking Press, 1961.

McGovern, James. *Crossbow and Overcast*. New York: William Morrow & Co., 1964.

Middlebrook, Martin. *The Peenemünde Raid*. London: Allen Lane, Penguin Books. 1982.

Minott, Rodney G. *The Fortress That Never Was*. New York: Holt, Rinehart & Winston, 1964.

Ordway, Frederick, and Sharpe, Mitchell. *The Rocket Team*. London: Heinemann, 1979.

Thomas, Shirley. *Men of Space*. Vol. 1. Philadelphia and New York: Chilton & Co., 1966

Williams, Beryl, and Epstein, Samuel. *Rocket Pioneers*. New York: Julian Messner, Inc., 1958

Articles and Documents

Bomber Command: The Air Ministry Account of Bomber Command's Offensive Against the Axis. London: His Majesty's Stationery Office, 1951.

The Army Air Forces in World War II. Vol. III, *Europe, January 1944 to May 1945*. Chicago: The University of Chicago Press, 1951.

"The History of Rocket Technology." In *Fourteen Essays on Research, Development and Utility.* Detroit: Wayne State University Press, 1964.

Handbook on Guided Missiles of Germany and Japan. Washington, D.C.: U.S. War Department, 1946.

The Story of Peenemünde: Interviews on German Rocket Research. Washington, D.C.: U.S. Army Air Forces, 1946.

Robertson, Terence. "The War Against von Braun." *MacLean's Magazine*, Canada, 1962.

Index